THE
SCOTTISH
DECISION

Also by Alan Hunter:
The Honfleur Decision

THE
SCOTTISH
DECISION

Alan Hunter

WALKER AND COMPANY
New York

First published in the United States of America in 1981 by the Walker Publishing Company, Inc.

ISBN: 0-8027-5456-2

Library of Congress Catalog Card Number: 81-51982

Printed in the United States of America

10 9 8 7 6 5 4 3 2 1

1

In the early hours of the morning of Tuesday August 22nd there was an explosion near the B851 road between Urchal and Daviot, Inverness-shire. It woke a farmer, Donald Geddes, of Ashtree Farm, about a mile distant; he started up in bed and, after a moment, shook his wife.

'Ailsie! Did you not hear that?'

'Ach, Donnie! What's there to hear?'

'There was a bang, woman. It sounded like a bomb.'

'Now who would be dropping bombs on Drummossie Muir ...'

'But I heard it, I tell you.'

'Ach, go to sleep. We've a heavy enough day coming on tomorrow.'

Nevertheless Geddes rose and went to the window to draw the curtains. In the dullness of first light he saw a column of black smoke strangely burnished with nettings of crimson.

'My God – it's a petrol fire. It must be a tanker that's blown up.'

'Donnie man ... come back to bed.'

'Woman, it'll be on our Long Pasture!'

Hastily Geddes pulled on clothes and went down to the Land Rover in the yard. The explosion had also woken his shepherd, James Cameron, who came running across from his cottage.

'Jump in man – there's trouble for certain.'

Together they slammed down the shadowy road. The fire, very fierce, was behind oak trees that fringed the long level of the moorland pasture. A gate stood ajar. Geddes turned in. They bounded and bumbled through the trees. Then they saw a shambles of white ash and twisted metal from which orange and crimson flame was towering.

'Almighty God ... a bluidy airplane!'

'There cannot be a soul alive in that ...'

Sobbing, keening, they leapt from the Land Rover and ran up and down before the wreck. But heat drove them back; an invisible wall, it kept them pinned at a distance of yards.

'Oh the poor bastards ... the poor bastards!'

'Search around Jamie – maybe some were thrown out.'

'They can not be living – no, they can not!'

'Search – search – there may be just one!'

Wildly they raced about the pasture, part lit by the dawn, part by the flames. Wrenched metal, debris were strewn about the area, but if there were bodies they found none.

'They're dead, Donnie, dead – let them be dead!'

'Oh God, the poor souls – pray God it was quick.'

'I dare not look longer – oh my heart!'

'A phone – let's get to a phone.'

Somehow Geddes drove back to the farmhouse, though his every limb was ashake. Babbling, he told of that blazing horror he had found behind trees on his Long Pasture. Stay with the incident, they told him, stay until our patrols get there. He swallowed whisky, got back in the Land Rover, but couldn't face the wreck again. He waited in the road.

At five-thirty p.m. on Tuesday 22nd the phone went in Gently's office. Distastefully he limbered it up: the voice was the Assistant Commissioner's.

'Drop what you're doing. I want you.'

In point of fact he'd been drawing a car. The latest of a long line, it sprawled ineptly across his desk pad. The car was a Deux-Chevaux; since he'd come back from France the cleaner had found batches of them in his waste basket – Deux-Chevaux drawn from every angle, but always with tall trees in the background.

Another thing since he had returned: he'd taken to coming out with phrases in French: phrases with a certain intonation, a cadence that he listened to while he spoke them ...

Irritably he tore off the Deux-Chevaux, crumpled it and sent it after the others.

'Sit, Gently.'

Two other men were already seated in the AC's office, one of them Empton, a Special Branch hawk between Gently and whom rapport was limited. The second man was a stranger, aged around forty, his face gaunt, deeply tanned. He stared hard at Gently. His clothes suggested un-English origin.

'Empton you know. Meet Superintendent Buchy of the French

DST.'

So that was it: Cartier's mob. No wonder Buchy was giving him the eye. The Frenchman rose and offered his hand.

'*Enchanté, monsieur.*'

'*Enchanté*'

'I have heard of you, it goes without saying, in connection with the affair of the terrorist Starnberg.'

'Bruno.'

'Indeed yes. Permit me to congratulate you, monsieur. In that encounter you displayed great gallantry, and I understand that an award is contemplated.'

'Though,' Empton said to no one, 'the grapevine has it that delight was tempered in certain quarters.'

Empton would be a buddy of Cartier's, naturally, thinking, probably acting like him. Buchy on the other hand seemed more civilised. One didn't see him shooting men through the head.

'Yes, well,' the AC said, giving his glasses a hitch. 'Your amazing exploits are fresh with everyone. Which is why you are here incidentally, and not because there's anything in it for you. But minister has spoken to minister and the can has descended to me. So tomorrow you fly north with Empton – and do your best to keep out of his hair.'

'I fly north ... ?'

'To Inverness.'

'Keeping out of my hair,' Empton said. 'That's the way the French want it, old man. You make such influential friends when you go abroad.'

No penny dropped. The AC took pity.

'Very briefly it goes like this. You impressed a top industrialist, one Hugo Barentin, who is related to a certain French minister. So now there's a flap on at Inverness and the cry goes up: "Send Gently".'

Still it didn ᐧnake sense. 'What flap?'

'Ah,' the AC said. He looked at Empton.

'Oh, tell him, sir,' Empton said. 'It'll hit the fan sooner or later.'

'Buchy, perhaps you will explain.'

Buchy gave a snap of his head. 'My dear colleague, it amounts to this. Unidentified agents have kidnapped Barentin.'

'Kidnapped him ... ?'

'He was ambushed, monsieur. Last night while driving home to

9

his château from Deauville. His car, a Rolls-Royce, was found parked on the verge with the chauffeur dead behind the wheel. Regrettably we were not informed until several hours after the event. A red-alert produced no results. We still await a message from his captors.'

'The PFLP?'

'Brilliant,' Empton said. 'It looks as though your heroics were wasted, old man. They failed to shoot him in July, so now they've kidnapped him in August.'

'They'll kill him.'

'*Ça va*. They're so damned un-British, old man. But they'll keep him alive for a time – until they've squeezed out the last drop of milk.'

Gently stared at nothing. Barentin! The man who had taken into his protection ... Still he could hear that voice, so dry, so leisurely, recall the sparse figure, feather-light with age. A spiritual man. A man willing to die for a vision of brotherhood between Jew and Arab ...

'What is it they want?'

Buchy shrugged. 'Until we hear from them we do not know. There are certain prisoners they wish to see freed, and Barentin is good for many millions. It may be they will deal directly with Tel Aviv for some political advantage.'

'But – if we know they'll kill him anyway?'

'Some arrangement may be offered that will save his life. But that is not in our hands, monsieur. Our brief is to locate him and to deal with his captors.'

'Before', Empton said, 'or perhaps after. Once he's dead they're cold meat.'

Buchy slid a glance at Empton, who smiled pleasantly and flicked his cuff. Empton had hard blue eyes, narrow features, high-bridged nose.

'But what has this to do with Inverness?'

'I'm glad you asked that,' Empton said. 'By now you can see that this is none of your business. You're just a cherry the French want on the cake.'

'Is Barentin in Scotland?'

'Full marks, old man.'

'Let me give you the picture,' the AC said. 'This morning the Inverness police were called out to a plane that apparently had crashed on Drummossie Muir. The wreck was located in a pasture beside a minor road leading to the A9. It was a complete burn-out. The police called out a team from RAF Kinloss. They found no bodies, identified the plane as a 10-seater Piper Chieftain, could discover no identification, satisfied themselves that the burning was deliberate. Enquiries were made with no result: no Piper Chieftain was overdue. But then we heard from Kinloss that they had found extra fuel-tanks, meaning that the plane could have come from outside. We checked round the compass. Paris had a Piper Chieftain overdue on a flight from Deauville to Marseilles. The times and place match. The plane would have taken off within an hour of Barentin's leaving the Yacht Club at Deauville. The wrecked plane still hasn't been identified, but we're hoping to get at it through engine serial numbers. Inverness police have found evidence of a car having been parked at the scene of the wreck.'

'We too have made enquiries,' Buchy said eagerly. 'That plane was bought recently by an ex-airline pilot. Last month he threw up his job with Air France and commenced in business as a charter-flyer. Where the money came from is not clear, but he is a man we have had our eye on before. He once flew charter for some people in Algeria who we suspected of drug and gun-running. He has a flat in Montparnasse and his name is Henri Hénault.'

'Hénault!'

Buchy paused. 'You have heard of him, monsieur?'

'His name – occurred – in the Starnberg case. But the Honfleur police checked him out.'

'None the less an interesting coincidence. What precisely was the connection?'

Gently's knuckles were white. 'He was formerly married to one of the ... one of the people involved.'

'Which one monsieur?'

It was ridiculous that he couldn't keep his calm! Empton's stoat-like eyes were on him, the AC peering, hand to glasses.

'One of the two women associated with Starnberg.'

'Ah yes – Mademoiselle Orbec. That was the one kept out of the case – at the instance, I believe, of Barentin himself.'

'She was unaware of Starnberg's identity.'

'I have no doubt of her innocence, monsieur. Yet the

coincidence stands. She was connected with Starnberg, and now we find her former husband involved with his colleagues.'

Damn the fellow!

'The situation was this. He could have been the gunman we were seeking. In the event he was shown to have been flying between Paris and Rio at the time of the incidents.'

'Yet ... some connection was suspected?'

'It was purely conjectural.'

'Go on old man,' Empton grinned. 'It gets amusing. When someone was potting at you, what made you think it was this lady's ex-husband?'

Gently said evenly: 'A theory was suggested by Inspector Frénaye of Honfleur. It was tested and found untenable. Hénault had no connection with the Starnberg case.'

Empton laughed scornfully. After a moment Buchy hoisted a shoulder.

'Very well then. Perhaps that is the case. But should we not have a word with Mademoiselle Orbec? It may be she has information about the associates of her ex-husband.'

Curse him!

'To my knowledge they have been separated for several years.'

'At the same time, if you have an address ...?'

'I know only that she lives in Rouen.'

He could feel sweat chill on his temples, the ache from his clenched hands. And they – they were missing nothing, eyeing him in a moment of silence. Suddenly the suppressed name blazed in his brain, making his eyes smart ... Gabrielle!

'I'd like to make a point if I may.'

'Please do,' the AC said.

'If in fact the PFLP have kidnapped Barentin, how likely is it that they would take him to Scotland?'

'Ah yes,' the AC said. 'That thought has been flitting through my mind too. At the moment we seem to be building unduly on our burned-out unidentified flying object. This Hénault has been a smuggler you say, but he has not yet been connected to international terrorism. I would find it easier to swallow a shipment of cannabis than a leading Zionist and his bloodthirsty captors.'

Buchy looked at Empton. Empton smiled distantly, then reached for a briefcase standing beside his chair. A pigskin affair, it had a combination lock which he spun with deft fingers. He took out a file. It was stamped SECRET, XXX. From the file he took a photograph. It showed, rather fuzzily, a bearded man in the act of getting into a car. Empton skimmed the photograph to the AC.

'McGash.'

'And who or what is McGash?'

'James Hector McGash.' Empton stretched out his legs, leaned back and took sight at the ceiling. 'Born Glasgow 1947, son of a respectable lawyer, educated Glasgow High School, LSE, Patrice Lumumba University, Moscow, and Lebanon. Associated with Starnberg code name Bruno in his later operations. A fixer, an accomplished tactician, man with a preference for neutralizing witnesses. Consequently we have but that one photograph, taken by chance in Paris.'

The AC quizzed the photograph blankly.

'The theory is that this man is involved?'

'Let's put it this way,' Empton said. 'If they wanted to hide Barentin in Scotland, they have a fixer who knows the ropes. And conversely, if Barentin is in Scotland, then McGash is the man we're dealing with.'

'Seems a back to front argument,' the AC said.

'But no,' Buchy said. 'Permit me to explain. Since the Starnberg affair last month there has been a big clean-up operation in France. We have raided many safe houses, made numerous arrests, impounded enough weapons to furnish an armoury. France at the moment is very hot for terrorists, and what happened to Starnberg will not have been forgotten.'

'It makes Scotland look a soft touch,' Empton said. 'Scots wha hae and shoot only at their legs. McGash will have contacts and local knowledge, and at the worst it will only be Come oot wi' yer hands oop.'

'Also,' Buchy said earnestly, 'is there not disaffection in Scotland?'

The AC stared over his glasses. He flipped the photograph to Gently. McGash showed as a powerfully built six-footer with broad-cheekboned features and large ears. He had a short thick neck and wiry pale hair. The mouth was lost in the beard. He was dressed in a light lounge suit and wore a billowing, loosely knotted tie.

'Then there is this laddie,' Empton said, producing another photograph from the file. 'Jamie's right-hand man, Yousef Hajjar. They were at Patrice Lumumba together.'

This time the photograph was posed. Hajjar was a slim, smiling man of medium height: narrow features, dark eyes, hatchet nose and coarse black hair.

'That's the team,' Empton said. 'They work together. Jamie proposes, Yousef disposes.'

'Well,' the AC said. 'You know your business. I'm merely here to follow instructions.'

'Which brings us back to France's choice,' Empton said. 'There really will be nothing for you to do, old man. I should take a fishing rod. There are trout in the Ness and they run a steamer trip down the loch.'

'Thank you,' Gently said.

The AC spread his hands. 'Probably good advice Gently,' he said. 'Treat it as a holiday. You haven't been yourself since you came back from France.'

Empton locked away his photographs. Buchy glanced at his watch. The AC rang Transport for a car to Heathrow. After shaking hands all round Buchy hesitated, then motioned Gently aside. He spoke in quick French.

'This Mademoiselle Orbec .. she enjoys a high level of protection ...?'

'She knows nothing.'

'Agreed. And I understand it is your wish ...?'

'She has suffered deeply.'

'Then that is enough. My dear colleague, may we meet again.'

He shook hands a second time, nodded to the others and left. Digging into his pockets, Empton said to the ceiling:

'Why don't the Frogs treat me like that?'

Gently took a tube to Finchley North and walked the difference to Elphinstone Road. He stared ahead, seeing no one, never glancing at the familiar pavements. In the Gardens kids were playing. Mrs Jarvis, his housekeeper, was chatting to a neighbour. He went straight through into his den and poured and drank a large whisky.

Gabrielle ...!

Pinned to the wall was Michelin map 55: Honfleur, Deauville-

Trouville, Cabourg, Lisieux ... Rouen. And names such as Pont l'Evêque, Villerville, Touques ... and that road that drew his eye like a magnet, running straight through the green shading of the forest. Near there, of necessity, they had snatched Barentin, most likely on the lightly used D62; they would have checked his route of an evening, found he avoided the busy coast road ...

'I've a nice bit of steak, Mr Gently. Would you like it with or without?'

Had he answered her? He was sitting now at his desk, apparently sinking his second whisky. Then he found himself sucking a dead pipe which he couldn't remember filling and lighting. And either he'd switched the light on, or Mrs Jarvis had done it for him ...

So after it had happened, in spite of Frénaye, he had rushed out to that hospital on the Pont l'Evêque road – Geoffrey had gone with him, and that had been lucky, since Frénaye had a gendarme posted in reception.

'Monsieur, you cannot be admitted ...'

'Monsieur, it is essential that I see her!'

'Monsieur, I have express orders ...'

That was when he would have hit him.

Presumably Geoffrey had got him away, and the next morning Frénaye had rung to say she had left the hospital. Saying nothing to the others, he'd rented a car and headed like a maniac down the Autoroute Normande. To Rouen ... to Rouen! The damned officials at the toll-gates had insisted he took his change – fighting, he'd won through the swirling traffic to the heart of the old city, to the Place Barthel. Her shop was larger than he'd imagined but inside were only assistants and Madame Glatigny:

'Oh Monsieur George, she is not here – and if she were she would not see you!'

'Where is she?'

'She has gone to Paris, and even to me she would give no address ...'

She was lying, he was sure of it. A directory, a street-map found him the house. Up in St-Aignan in a steep, quiet road ... for minutes he'd kept his thumb on the bell. Nothing, nothing, nothing! Then he'd sat watching through the whole afternoon, gone back to stare at the now-shuttered shop, to limp home again to Honfleur, Equemauville ...

She'd gone. And suddenly Normandy was a vacuum he could scarcely bear. Honfleur, Lisieux, the rest, she had taken their soul with her when she went. He couldn't bear it ... but he couldn't leave it! Each day he'd gone down to the old town, hung about the harbour, the basin, the Place Ste-Catherine, his heart pumping at the sight of every green Deux-Chevaux. In love there were miracles, she had said. Could there not be a miracle now? To pluck from her heart those intolerable memories that, in the evening of that day, she'd felt unable to live with ...?

But the green Deux-Chevaux were never her Deux-Chevaux, no more she came running across the Place Ste-Catherine. Geoffrey painted his pictures, Bridget went her pilgrimages, and one day they were on the ferry slipping out of Dieppe. It couldn't end there! That miracle must happen! He'd stood watching the stooping cliffs fade to haze. Then the wake, stretching back to France, the last, tenuous link between him and her ...

'It's ready for you, Mr Gently.'

'A moment!'

He was searching in his desk for the telephone codebook. Rouen was now STD, while in his notebook a scribbled number ...

'Hullo ... yes?'

It was Madame Glatigny.

'Madame, it's me. You *must* let me speak to her!'

'Oh Monsieur George, if only you could. But, in any case, she is not here.'

'Isn't there ...?'

'No, monsieur. She has gone I know not where. This morning early she had a phone call, then she packed a bag and left.'

'But ... she must have said where?'

'No. No. Monsieur knows how it is with mademoiselle. I ask her of course, but she says it is personal, that she will be back in a few days.'

'Madame ... did she take her passport?'

'Monsieur, I could not say.'

'Do you know where she keeps it?'

'Oh yes.'

'Madame, I would be obliged if you would check whether it is gone.'

Followed harmonics. Tense, blank faced, Gently sat sniffing a faint odour of grilled steak. He daren't let himself think! In

Elphinstone Road, lights suddenly blinked above the pavements.

'Monsieur?'

'Yes?'

'It is not here.'

'Ah!'

More harmonics.

'Monsieur, may I say you must not hope that it is to England that she goes.'

'Madame Glatigny—'

'Oh monsieur! Mademoiselle has been so very unhappy. I am hoping always that she will reconsider, but I do not think that time is yet.'

'Madame, with regard to the phone call—'

'Monsieur, at the time I was in the bathroom.'

'Thank you madame.'

'Oh Monsieur George, I pray that one day all shall be well.'

He hung up and went to eat his steak. Having served it, Mrs Jarvis returned to her television. He ate stolidly, the background to his thoughts a wailing voice with interruptions of applause.

'Frenchie,' the bearded man had said, 'there's no going back to France for you, man. If they believed you, which they won't, you'd still be in for a long stretch. So make up your mind, Frenchie boy. It's us who hold the key to Fort Knox. At the end of this caper we'll be flying out, and we'd sooner have a peelo who doesn't need a gun on him.'

'But of course, Jamie,' he'd said. 'Did I not come in with my eyes open? What it was about I did not care, and for such payment I would shoot my grandmother.'

'Aye, stick to that, Frenchie,' the bearded man had said. 'Just think of that million dollars in Aden. And whist! A word in your ear – you must not cross Dusty at any rate. He's a real nasty man, Frenchie, who would sooner blast you than share a hot dinner. You'll bear that in mind?'

'I'll bear it in mind, Jamie.'

'Aye,' the bearded man had said. 'Then I doubt you'll do.'

Much later they had passed a village with a shop and the bearded man had ordered Dusty to stop. He had taken out a written list and peeled English money from a wad.

'Now Frenchie, my man, you're a French tourist – they're used

17

to such cattle round here. Just ask them to put up what's on the list – and never act edgy. There's no cry out yet.'

He had taken the list and money, crossed the parking and entered the shop. So early, the shop was empty and attended only by one woman.

'Madame ... miss ...?'

She had taken his list smilingly and begun to place items on the counter. The shop, which was also a post office, had a public phone at the back.

2

At noon on Wednesday 23rd they were in the circuit above Dalcross Airport, with Moray Firth sun-dusted below and Inverness sharp beyond a wing tip. South west one could see the Great Fault stretching away to the pale smudge of Fort Augustus at the head of the loch, then on through blue hills to infinity and at last the Atlantic. The cleft that split Scotland in two: was it surprising that legend clung to it? Even seen from the seat of an aircraft it inspired a sensation of the uncanny. A geological flashpoint, half-sleeping potential ... in that deep trough might not mysteries remain?

Superintendent Guthrie, porridgy, beaming, came forward to meet them at reception. He shook hands with a hearty clasp and hurried them through to a waiting Jaguar. As they sped away from the airport he twisted round to face Empton.

'Are we any the forwarder, then, on this job?'

Empton gave him a blue stare. 'First, old man, if you don't mind, we'll hear what the locals have been up to.'

'Ach ... well.' Guthrie glanced at Gently, who met him with wooden face. The local man had pale, jowled features and a clipped accent, perhaps of Edinburgh origin. 'You'll understand we have been working in the dark, with not so much as a description of the men we're seeking. Furthermore we've no clue to where they might have been heading. For all we know they could be in England.'

'Not,' Empton said, 'in England. Just take my word for that, old man.'

'Well then,' Guthrie said. 'Suppose they're in Scotland, it is not like alerting the home counties. Here our men are thin on the ground, and much of the country without roads. If they've taken to Knoydart, for example, or The Parph, or A'Mhoine, they could declare independence for all we'd hear of it.'

'But meanwhile,' Empton said, 'they have a car, old man, and a tactical need to use a telephone. So let's forget the Celtic Twilight and hear what you've been doing where they speak English.'

Guthrie flashed Gently another look. 'There has been a general alert,' he said. 'We assumed that these men did not arrive here by accident and that they had a safe house waiting. In consequence we have been checking rented property, hotels and boarding houses. Also remote farms and such as shooting-lodges, where occupation is occasional.'

'Excellent,' Empton said. 'And by way of results?'

Guthrie merely shut his mouth tight. They were speeding along beside the Firth, across which, in the distance, rose cloud-dappled hills.

'Well, well, old man,' Empton said. 'We must try to put things on a more hopeful footing. Which, be it known, is why I'm here. With full Home Office authority, it goes without saying.'

'We shall cooperate,' Guthrie said through his teeth.

'Yes,' Empton said. 'I think so, old man. I'm playing a game for rather high stakes, so we'll just take cooperation for granted.'

'And your colleague?' Guthrie said, nodding to Gently.

'Ah, I'm glad you mentioned him,' Empton said. 'I want a little leak to the local press saying that he's here to study Scottish police procedure.'

Guthrie gaped. 'But why should we do that? His presence here requires no explanation.'

'Brilliant,' Empton said. 'But follow orders, old man. That way we'll all know what we're doing.'

Guthrie clamped his mouth shut again. They navigated a roundabout and entered Inverness by a ramshackle street. Then they were creeping with massed traffic down the broad, much lane-marked High Street. Guthrie jerked round to Gently.

'I'll just say this,' he said. 'I'm at sea in this matter, and I admit it. But if you are Chief Superintendent Gently, then I ken a man who kens you. That's Superintendent Sinclair, as he now is, who runs his show up in Dornoch. Perhaps you recall him?'

'I recall him,' Gently said.

'Aye. And a good word he puts in for you. So you're welcome here, man, to Inverness, whatever daft doings they've sent you up for.'

'Thank you,' Gently said.

'Ha, ha,' Empton said. 'I went to Winchester, myself.'

Guthrie's neck looked a little pink. They made a left turn towards the Castle.

Guthrie led them into an incident room which however seemed singularly devoid of incidents. Two men sat manning phones, a third rose from a desk as they entered.

'Inspector Tate,' Guthrie said. 'He's i/c of the operation.'

Empton ignored him. He went to the desk, sat, unlocked his briefcase and produced the photographs. These today included one of Hénault, at a glimpse a good-looking man with a pencilled moustache. Then, from a separate file, he took a press photo of Barentin. He spread the photographs on the desk and added some sheets of printed particulars.

'To be copied and circulated,' he said. 'For a start to every police station within a hundred mile radius.'

Guthrie gulped. 'Have a heart, man,' he said. 'We don't have the facilities here that you're used to in London.'

'For a start,' Empton said. 'Meaning this afternoon. I don't think you appreciate the urgency, old man. By tomorrow morning I want this lot circulated to every police station north of the Tweed.'

'But we can never do it!'

'Oh, I think so,' Empton said. 'Cooperation, old man. Chop-chop.'

Silence for a moment. Then Tate motioned to a phone-watcher, who took the photographs and left. Empton smiled cheerfully and took yet another file from his briefcase.

'Let's put it in focus, shall we?' he said. 'Up till now I feel the response has been rather tentative. You've been treating this as one of your amateur crimes, which it most distinctly is not.'

'If you're accusing us of slackness—' Guthrie began.

'Yes,' Empton said. 'Don't interrupt, old man. I'm here to talk, you're here to listen, tax payers' money and all that.' He drew a typed sheet from the file. 'This came in from Paris last night,' he said. 'The ungodly have been in touch with the Quai D'Orsay through the good offices of a certain wog lawyer. Seven releases, four in France, two in Germany, one in Holland, twenty million dollars to accounts in Aden, plane and safe conduct to Algiers. About—' he fanned himself with the document '—what our colleagues had been expecting.'

Guthrie's eyes had rounded. 'That's—that's their demand?' he said.

'For the safe return of Barentin,' Empton said. 'But of course they're certain to kill him.'

'Twenty million dollars!'

'Inflation, old man. They used to be content with five or ten.'

'But that's preposterous!'

'Barentin can pay it. The meat in the sandwich is the seven releases.' Empton's eyes bored at Guthrie. 'Not an amateur crime is it, old man? So forget the Stone of Scone and Great Train Robberies, we're in the Premier League here. Our business is to track, find and neutralize and to be otherwise un-British. We're outside the cosy world of Magna Carta. Here we don't ask questions even afterwards.'

Guthrie stared. 'You can't mean that.'

Empton's teeth showed white. 'Sorry to shock you, old man,' he said. 'But it's time you learned what you have on your plate. I want those men. I prefer them dead. I am not in the least concerned about Barentin. And now we've got that out of the way, perhaps we can descend to business.'

'You'd actually – shoot them?'

'Yes,' Empton said. 'Please give your attention, old man. That message to Paris tells us something. Our men are almost certainly on the end of a phone.'

Guthrie looked sick. He pulled up a chair. Tate remained standing, his eyes fascinated. The remaining phone-watcher was talking thick Scots to a colleague reporting in from Achnasheen. From a gold case Empton took and lit a straw-coloured cigarette.

'Now,' he said. 'Small deductions. Routine ploys are out. McGash knows better than you do where the police begin a search. He knows the country, has at least one agent, the man who relays calls to Paris. He's inside a hundred miles from the wreck because it wouldn't have paid him to have driven much further. Suggestions?'

'To go north,' Tate ventured, 'he'd have to drive through the town, sir.'

'A map.'

Tate hurriedly found one. Empton spread it on the desk and studied it.

'Go on.'

'East is lowlands, sir, he wouldn't find so much cover there. South, he'd have to take the main A9. To my mind he would have stayed with the B851.'

'Ah,' Empton said. 'Down the loch. What sort of coun'ry is it over there?'

'Fairly well populated, sir, between the loch and the Monadhliath Hills.'

'But then he's through west,' Guthrie said. 'With plenty of glens and nooks to choose from. A hundred miles would take him into Kintail, or up by Garry, or Arkaig.'

'Right,' Empton said. He exhaled smoke. 'I want an operation in all that sector. From Daviot here down the loch into Kintail as far as Shiel Bridge. I want it combed to the last shieling, in fact particularly the last shieling. Because, old man, that's where we'll find them – not in hotels or bed-and-breakfasts.'

'But that'll take weeks,' Guthrie said. 'You'd need an army.'

'No, I think not,' Empton said. 'Because why? Because they need a telephone, and where there isn't a telephone we needn't search. Start at a phone box, work outwards. Check with shops adjacent to phones. They need to eat, will want to buy the papers, may have to replenish gas, petrol, paraffin.' He sucked pensively. 'With regard to shooters, I think we should make an issue, old man. Damned un-British and all that, but probably better than a lot of dead policemen. McGash will have Czech M52's most likely, a darling weapon that can shoot through bricks.'

'I'll have to get special authorization,' Guthrie said thickly.

'Use the phone old man,' Empton said. 'And now, if you don't mind, I'd like my lunch. We'll spread the net further this afternoon.'

He stubbed his cigarette and rose. Guthrie rose. Tate moved aside. Gently withdrew from a window where he'd been staring at the Ness flowing darkly below. Guthrie looked at Gently.

'And the Superintendent?' he said to Empton.

'Ah yes,' Empton said. 'Speaking of angels. I'm afraid all this bores the Superintendent. Perhaps you could amuse him with the loan of a car.'

Guthrie looked at a loss.

'Thank you,' Gently said. 'If you can spare a car I shall be grateful.'

'But of course man, of course,' Guthrie said.

'Now,' Empton said, 'everybody's happy.'

They were booked in at a hotel across the river and almost opposite the castle. Along each bank of the Ness stretched a tree-lined promenade beyond which rose buildings in pinkish-red sandstone. Square, generous Victorian dwellings, firmly quoined in the Scottish taste, with a church or two of the same material, notched against green slopes and far, brooding hills. The Ness was wide, swift and shallow. A delicate suspension bridge crossed it for pedestrians. Two anglers, up to their crotches, were patiently whipping the town reach.

Gently ate fresh salmon, salad, a wedge of Black Forest gateau. Across from him Empton had nothing to say. His blue stare was turned continually across the river, as though X-raying the police station and the progress of its inmates. Finally, when the coffee came, he lit a cigarette and stared at Gently.

'Forty-eight hours, old man,' he said. 'Perhaps sooner if I crack the whip and get the natives off their arses.'

Gently said nothing. Empton leached smoke.

'A pity about you, old man,' he said. 'So much talent and moral rectitude. Metropolitan's loss and nobody's gain.'

'I know Barentin,' Gently said.

'Please,' Empton said, 'no appeal to my sentiments. I haven't got any. Barentin's cold meat. They'll take him with them if they make their point and deliver a body at Algiers. Or shoot him if I make mine. Either way he's a dead duck.'

'A conditional deal,' Gently said. 'Hold one of theirs to swop at Algiers.'

'Yes, interesting,' Empton said. 'But I didn't come with tickets to Algiers.'

'Then a hostage swop.'

'Not McGash.'

'Perhaps for me,' Gently said.

Empton stared at him through smoke, blue eyes puckered curiously.

'Yes, possible,' he said. 'In fact, intriguing. The cop who neutralised his old chum Bruno. McGash might just buy that. But it'd be corpse for corpse, old man.'

'That's my risk.'

Empton stared on. 'What makes you tick, old man?' he said.

'I've never known. You surprised Cartier. He's still grieving over that report.'

'But if I'm willing?'

Slowly Empton shook his head. 'Read the scenario again, old man. This is a clean job. No loose ends. I'm here to make honest men of terrorists.'

'There aren't any clean jobs.'

'Ha, ha,' Empton said. 'Now let's sing Rule Britannia.'

Guthrie came in. He was sweating slightly.

'I've fetched your car, man,' he said to Gently. He produced keys. 'Down in the yard. A Marina was the best I could do.'

'Brilliant choice,' Empton said. 'Brilliant.'

Guthrie ignored him and signalled a waiter. Empton finished his cigarette, rose, clicked his heels, left.

'I could murder that bastard,' Guthrie said. 'Maybe I will do before it's over. Are there many like him?'

Gently shrugged. 'He's probably the best man we've got.'

'He's twisted,' Guthrie said. 'My God, he frightens me. He makes me frightened of myself. If he's the way things are going then we're really on the skids.' He downed a fruit juice. 'But you, man – where do you come into his game?'

'I don't,' Gently said. He explained. Guthrie listened with intent eyes.

'Aye,' he said. 'I can understand that, with you knowing this Barentin too. So you're supernumerary?'

'In a word.'

'My gosh, man, I wish it was you at the helm. Then what will you be doing?'

Gently sucked an empty pipe. One of the anglers had just hooked a trout.

He rang home. He had alerted Mrs Jarvis to the possible arrival of a message – phone, letter, word of mouth: he couldn't be certain what it would be. But there was no message. He left his address, hung up, brooded, dialled International Exchange. It took time to get a line to Honfleur, but time was something he had in handfuls. At last:

'Gendarmerie d'Honfleur?'

It was a voice he recognised: Bocasse.

'Superintendent Gently.'

'Ah, monsieur! I am happy to hear your voice.'

'You have recovered, Monsieur Bocasse.'

'But yes, I am out of the hospital two, three weeks. They were but flesh wounds, monsieur, scratches. It is kind of monsieur to enquire.'

'I wish to speak to Inspector Frénaye.'

'Monsieur, I am desolate, but he is on leave. He will be heartbroken to have missed you, and meanwhile, if I can be of assistance ...'

'When will he be back?'

'Not till Monday, monsieur. But, as I say—'

'Did he leave a number?'

'No, monsieur. I regret that I cannot tell how to reach him.'

He'd had a bottle sent up to his room and now he broached it and poured a stiff one. Had he really believed she would come to England, that somehow this nightmare of longing was ending? Perhaps Frénaye could have told him something; Frénaye, he knew, had been to talk to her. On some official business in Rouen he'd made time to visit the shop in the Place Barthel. But then, reporting it, he had been cagey, referring to it merely as a casual visit ... because he knew the affair was hopeless? In a flash, the scene in the forest flared before Gently's eyes ...

He drank, sat crouched over the glass. Now he was forcing himself to see it again: the wrecked cars, bleeding body, gas dispersing through the trees. And her distorted face, her hooked hands as he sought to come between it and her ... the horror, the loathing in her eyes. And Cartier, with his gun ...

That was what lay between them: the moment that led to her despair. The moment she had tried to destroy in oblivion in the dark waters of the harbour. And yet ...

He rose and went over to the window, stared hard at the scene without. Surely it couldn't be for ever, that initial reaction of despair? She wasn't to blame. She had been manipulated: nothing she had done could count against her. Even the belief they had tricked her into had been quickly eroded by judgement, by love ... All was forgiveable. Yet, dully, he understood that such a spirit as hers wouldn't brook forgiveness, not from him, not from herself: from herself least of all. *Impasse* impossible: if in love there were miracles, no less was needed to untie this knot. Gabrielle ...! Where was she now – in all the world, where was she?

Restlessly he turned from the window, commenced tramping up and down. That telephone call! From whom had it come, to send her at once to pack her bag? Her father, her mother were dead, and she had no close relatives that he knew of. Hénault? Was there a connection? He paused in his stride, but shook his head. He had heard her speak of him: all that was long over: that she would be involved in his affairs was unthinkable. Then ... a friend, perhaps a friend in trouble? That was more the style of Gabrielle! And if out of France then most likely in London, where she had spent a year at the time of her divorce ...

He splashed and gulped more whisky: in London, where she would expect him to be! Perhaps not intending, not wishing to see him, but – in London: in his city. And once there, mustn't that fact work on her, softening her, suggesting possibilities, at last planting in her heart the impossibility of leaving without some motion, some gesture towards him? But he, he was no longer there, no longer waiting to respond to the gesture: though the whole wide city vibrated with her presence he was out on a limb in Inverness ...

And suddenly the northern sun was cold, the distant hills an oppression. What was he doing here? Barentin, had he known, would at once have urged him to return to town. Which he could not, useless as he was! Getting drunk was the last option open.

Disgusted with himself, he slammed down the glass and went down out of the hotel. Something he must do, if he stayed there, other than brooding in his room. He went to look at the car. It had a full tank and the clock showed less than nine thousand. But after sitting in it for a spell he relocked it and set out on foot to the police station.

And that too was a frost, as he sensed it would be the moment he set foot through the door. Empton, having set the place in a turmoil, had cleared off on a reconnaissance down the loch. Guthrie meanwhile had returned to a routine seriously hampered by Empton's exactions, and Tate was furiously typing up a check list of information coming in. No room for Gently! Though Tate politely rested on his keys when Gently came in.

'Anything stirring?'

'Nothing yet, sir. Just two bottles of liquid methane.'

'Two what?'

Tate's eyes were lively. He was a lean, neat man with a clipped moustache.

'Two of our men found some interesting apparatus in a barn not far from Errogie. It might have been mistaken for a whisky still, but the owner explained that it was for reducing methane gas to a liquid. Our men took a couple of sample bottles, which they intend to examine at Hogmanay.'

'And that's it?'

Tate made a face, sighed and went back to rattling the keys.

Trying to get into the act somewhere, Gently stumped over to the big wall map. What he had to do was get her out of his mind, to think, to behave again like a policeman. To remember Barentin, however little he could help him – Barentin, whom Empton had written off as cold meat. At least to check and recheck their thinking: some detail of significance might yet emerge ...

But the thinking was sound. McGash, unless devious, would almost certainly have taken the direction predicted. He had nothing to gain by risking the town, seeking the lowlands, or heading down the A9. Behind the loch he had quiet, direct roads to the western glens and even Skye ... onwards, northwards if he chose, or into such backlands as Knoydart, Ardnamurchan. And if he were devious? Then prediction was useless: one could but circulate the details widely. Which Empton was doing. You couldn't fault him. And the map suggested nothing but what was being done.

'Some more info, sir ...'

It was pathetic – Tate doing his best to make Gently feel wanted!

'Was there a Press release?'

'The Super gave them a ring, sir, just to let them know you were in town.'

And that was his usefulness expended. To keep face he'd glanced over the sheets of Tate's check list – in their way, a curious sidelight into the everyday life of the area. But then he'd retreated, tail between legs, the least wanted man in Inverness ...

After which nothing, a period of blankness, tramping the streets of Inverness, watching the traffic stream over the bridge to divide right for the north or press on to the west: a blank that ended finally when he found himself clutching a phone.

'Any message for me ...?'

'No, Mr Gently ... just a thing from the RAC.'

'No phone calls?'

'A Mr Simpson who wanted to talk about insurance ...'

It was time to eat, so he ate; this time splendidly alone. Empton doubtless was still cracking his whip, whether up the glen or in Guthrie's stronghold. At the next table there was a French party, a mother, father, three teenage children: they laughed and jested together, and one of the girls, seen in profile ...

How long could he take it? Inverness was a limbo growing more unreal as the hours passed. A town he'd dropped into out of the sky, an island of nowhere surrounded by nothing. His body was here but his soul was in London: and this was only the first day. Tomorrow there'd be morning, noon and night ... and then another day ... perhaps another ...

Rather than face the temptation of the bottle he strode out again into the town. Dusk was gathering and lights were strung along each bank of the black river. He walked beside it, past the modern cathedral, past the ultra-modern theatre; crossed the swaying suspension bridge, which bounced underfoot like a trampoline. On every side there were couples, men and women: he, merely a ghost passing among them! While night grew blacker about the sparkling town and hardened the shapes of far-off hills.

'... had a relaxing evening, old man?'

Some trick of time found him back in reception – much later, it must have been, since lights had been turned off in the dining room. Then there was Empton collecting his key, a cigarette trailing from the twist of his mouth.

'Any progress ...?'

'Would you care, old man?'

But he didn't want to talk to Empton. The bar was still open: he went through, caught the barman in the act of checking his till.

'A double!'

'Mr Gently, sir ...?'

'Well?'

The barman nodded towards the shadows. A man who'd been sitting there had risen and was coming towards them.

The man was Frénaye.

3

'*Monsieur!*'

'*Monsieur!*'

At that moment unreality seemed complete. Inverness had dissolved, become a mirage, a place reserved for the totally improbable. But Frénaye was real. He came forward with his familiar, apologetic smile, the tender, dark eyes, the warm, half-embarrassed handshake. And for some reason Gently glanced back into reception to check whether Empton's eyes were on them.

'Monsieur, this is absurdly unexpected!'

'Monsieur, I am stupidly happy to see you!'

'But how—?'

'It is easily explained.'

'Barman, a double scotch for my friend!'

Frénaye was colouring, shyly delighted at the impression he had created. Dressed informally in blazer and slacks, he looked anything but an Inspector of Police. For an instant they gazed at each other, wordless. Then the barman handed the drinks.

'Your health!'

'And yours, monsieur.'

'But where are you staying?'

'In this same hotel.'

'With madame and your family?'

'Not ... exactly.'

'Then?'

Frénaye shrugged awkwardly. 'It is easily explained.'

But almost he didn't want an explanation, would have preserved the emotion of the moment: this sudden, it must be significant, contact with a world that was his and hers. Inverness, from being unreal, had exploded into sharp definition, a place vitally important, quite unrecognizable as the desert of ten minutes ago.

'Let's go to my room ... have you eaten?'

'In fact, I have missed several meals.'

'Barman, the best they can do!'

'I have been travelling you understand ... I set out this morning.'

Still he didn't want to hear it at once. He hustled Frénaye up to his room – a room that had changed utterly from the chamber of wretchedness he had slammed the door on. And Frénaye, he too seemed reluctant to volunteer details – was suffering no doubt from fatigue, compounded by lack of nourishment. But the latter was soon put right: a tray was quickly delivered to the room. Sitting rather comfortlessly at a bedside table, Frénaye tucked away cold pie and salad and apple tart. Then Gently's mood became one of impatience, he could scarcely wait for Frénaye to finish. At last the Frenchman drank his coffee and shyly took out his pipe.

'My first meal since breakfast, monsieur.'

'But why? What sent you dashing up here?'

'I had due to me a few days' leave ...'

'Oh come on! Why to Inverness?'

Frénaye puffed self-consciously. 'It is simple really ... your colleagues informed me where I could find you. In fact, I tried to phone you yesterday, but at the time you were out.'

'So immediately you jump on a plane?'

'I phoned again this morning. Then they tell me you have come up here, and so, as I say, having leave due ...'

'But why?'

Frénaye looked embarrassed; he puffed and avoided Gently's eye. 'It is this way, monsieur. I was going to ask you a question about a certain person you have heard of.'

'Who I have – heard of?'

'Exactly, monsieur. Whose name came up when you were in France. It has come to my knowledge that this person is in trouble, in short has urgent need of assistance.'

Gently stared. 'Are we talking of Barentin?'

'Barentin?' Frénaye also stared. 'No, monsieur, not Barentin, though of course I am aware of that terrible business. It need not be said that I was involved in the initial search and inquiry, but the affair was quickly taken over by the DST, and then a security clamp was imposed.'

'Who then?'

'I am afraid I may distress you. The man we are speaking of is Henri Hénault.'

'Hénault!'

'I would not, in normal circumstances—'

'But Hénault flew the plane for the kidnappers!'

Now they were staring at each other – Frénaye with mouth slightly agape! After a pause he rose and went to puff his pipe at the window.

'This is – certain?'

'Quite certain. The kidnapping is the reason why I am here.'

'Hénault has been arrested?'

'Not yet. But there is an intensive search in progress. Hénault flew them out from Deauville-Trouville to a rendezvous here. The plane was burnt. They had twelve hours grace before anyone tumbled to what had happened.'

'And you are ... in charge?'

Gently laughed ironically. 'I'm here on request, because of Starnberg. The man in charge is Chief Superintendent Empton, who you may have seen me speaking to in reception.'

Frénaye puffed a few more times before returning to his chair. He seemed at a loss; at last he gestured, turned to Gently with troubled eyes.

'Monsieur, my position is difficult – in fact, more delicate than I had supposed. If I had known this morning what I know now, I think I would still be in France.'

'Would a drink help?'

'I would be most grateful.'

Gently poured and handed a glass. By now he also had his pipe goiing and they sipped and puffed in unison. But still Frénaye was hesitating.

'So you have information,' Gently prompted.

Slowly, Frénaye nodded. 'That, monsieur, is the problem. It is information critical in more ways than one, and I am in doubt if I should reveal it. What I am seeking in my mind's eye, monsieur, is very much what you saw in the Forêt de St-Gatien. And if that comes about, then I fear greatly for Monsieur Barentin's safety. What sort of man is your Superintendent Empton?'

'One of Cartier's breed,' Gently shrugged.

'Then you understand. Yet, notwithstanding, I cannot entirely ignore my duty. Monsieur, would it be possible to regard this communication as unofficial?'

Gently puffed. 'Let me put it this way. I'll do nothing that might increase Monsieur Barentin's peril.'

'You will not necessarily inform this Empton?'

'As much and no more as you would inform Cartier.'

Frénaye nodded gratefully. 'Then that is satisfactory. Yet one condition I must insist on. This information came to me confidentially, and you must not insist that I reveal the source.'

Gently stared hard at him: Frénaye's eyes didn't falter.

'Very well.'

'Thank you, monsieur.' Frénaye took a gulp from his glass, sucked once or twice at a dead pipe. 'So then. It comes to my knowledge that Hénault is mixed up in some criminal enterprise, the seriousness of which he did not know when he agreed to it. Once implicated, he cannot withdraw, but is obliged to accompany his criminal colleagues, who have promised him a large sum of money for his part in the crime. Nevertheless, he is strongly of the opinion that he will be paid not in gold but in lead, and he takes an opportunity to communicate his plight and to implore assistance. Monsieur, we now know the nature of the enterprise, and can estimate the reality of his fears.'

Gently grunted. 'And that's all?'

'Not quite monsieur.' Frénaye jigged his shoulders. 'But, if I may, I would emphasize those two points, that Hénault is partly innocent and that his peril is far from imaginary. It appears that he has lulled his colleagues' suspicions by a display of advidity and enthusiastic cooperation, but of course they do not trust him as one of themselves and any false move is likely to be fatal. His situation is desperate, monsieur, and his cry for help equally penetrating.'

Gently sat silent for a few moments. Nervously, Frénaye relit his pipe. Below, in the riverside drive, a few late cars were drifting by. At intervals, because the window was open, one could hear the faint lisp of a freshet in the river. Not looking at Frénaye, Gently said:

'You know where they are.'

Frénaye sighed, but said nothing.

'Well?' Gently said.

'Monsieur ... I would remind you ... I came here ignorant of the nature of Hénault's involvement. From his record smuggling was suspected – which indeed is an offence sufficiently serious – but the whole facts are not known. And monsieur's presence here did not suggest them.'

'But you know where they are.'

'If I may put it this way. I can perhaps indicate a certain area. Also, it may be that I have a clue which, to the knowledgeable, will suggest a location. That, monsieur, at the moment, is the extent of my information.'

'At the moment?'

Frénaye shrugged and merely went on puffing. His face was a little flushed and wearing a mulish expression. Gently picked up the bottle and replenished the glasses; Frénaye acknowledged with a slight gesture.

'Look,' Gently said. 'I'm not a fool, and you know I'm not a fool. If Hénault got to a phone the odds are high that he would ring a certain person. And that certain person might phone you in the hope of your knowing what was going on. And you began ringing me and found that I'd gone to Inverness. And now you're here – with information that could, and should, have gone through the usual channels.'

'Monsieur, I cannot stop you thinking—'

'She came to Scotland – that's why you're here! She listened to that no-good ex-husband of hers and went off to try to get him out of his scrape. And you didn't split, you came chasing after her to keep her out of trouble – and perhaps to head her off from me, in case there was a danger of collision! Where is she, Frénaye?'

'But, monsieur—!'

'Is she here in Inverness?'

'Monsieur, I must remind you of the condition —'

'Listen Frénaye, she's playing with fire.'

'Monsieur, to the best of my knowledge—'

'I must know where she is.'

Hot-faced, Frénaye set his lips tight.

'Then – I go to Empton.'

'No monsieur – no!'

Gently was on his feet, stalking up and down. Anguishedly, Frénaye jumped up and seized Gently by the arm.

'Calm yourself monsieur – please, please!'

'Monsieur, she is in deadly danger.'

'Monsieur, you do not think what you may be doing —'

'Then where is she?'

'Monsieur, calm yourself – please! – and listen.'

Gently groaned and threw himself back on his chair. He grabbed up his glass and drained it. Frénaye straightened his blazer, sat, edged his chair closer to Gently's.

'Monsieur, if you go to this Empton I shall deny everything, make no mistake. There is only safety for Barentin while his captors feel themselves secure. There may be a chance, perhaps a small one, that negotiations will succeed, and I, Maurice Frénaye, will do nothing to put them in jeopardy.'

'Although, meanwhile—'

'Meanwhile, monsieur, I am bound by a promise which I may not break. But this I can tell monsieur, that, while admitting nothing, I can assure him that no foolish risks are being taken. There is perhaps a waiting game in progress, with a listening post in the enemy camp. Opportunities may arise, who knows? But not if monsieur makes a foolish blunder.'

'At least tell me where she is!'

'Monsieur, I admit nothing.'

'Do you deny she is involved?'

'I will neither deny nor admit, but remind monsieur that I laid down a condition which he accepted.'

Frénaye was trembling slightly and a gleam showed on his flushed face. But his gentle eyes were determined and his singing French had become staccato. Useless to push him ... and yet, he knew! As sure as they sat there Gently was convinced of it. Out there in the dark jewelled town or in the near or distant hills – at a spot on which Frénaye could put his finger – sharing the same stars: Gabrielle! Gabrielle, running risks of a magnitude of which she had no conception ...

'Monsieur ... dare I speak of a certain person?'

'I know she left France, Frénaye.'

'Monsieur I have talked to her on several occasions in addition to the one I saw fit to report. She has in fact been twice to Honfleur, once spending the weekend with myself and madame my wife. That occasion, I may now reveal, was while monsieur was yet in France.'

'She was in the town!'

Blood rushed to his cheeks: he could feel the thump of it in his ears. Then ... she had been so near in the nightmare of those last few days!

'Why didn't you tell me?'

'Impossible monsieur.'

'At least – a hint!'

Frénaye shook his head sadly. 'It would have made bad worse, monsieur, and perhaps have been disastrous to mademoiselle. She was in a state of great depression and uncertainty. I feared that she might repeat her rash act.'

'But ... when all was explained?'

'It was not explained, monsieur, or not to the mind of mademoiselle. What she saw in the forest had unhinged her. She wished to believe, but at first she dared not.'

'You could have reassured her!'

'Monsieur, I tried. It was for that she came to me in her distress. Monsieur, I talked to her, I swore many lies to get that dangerous impression out of her brain. Yet still you could see in her eyes it remained, she was living it again and again. She was seeing Cartier shooting Starnberg through the head with, it appeared, your entire approbation.'

Gently groaned. Yes, like that it must have seemed, while still she was supposing him a man of violence. But afterwards, when the truth was told, when she understood the misrepresentation ...? Even then, apparently, that searing image could not be cast out by a babble of assurance ...

'What did you tell her?'

Frénaye's hands rose and fell. 'That monsieur was a man for whom such things were impossible. That I had known you for years, that I had seen your service record, that you were the respected friend of Monsieur Barentin. Also I told her you had filed a report on the basis of which there would be an inquiry, that Cartier would certainly be punished and yourself perhaps called as a prosecution witness. But at first all this was in vain. She heard me and wept. It was pitiable, monsieur.'

'And then ...?'

'She came again, monsieur, and implored me to tell her these things once more. This time she listened without weeping and asked me many question. Then she told me something not included in your report, a confused memory that had returned to her. She thought that at some point you approached Cartier, took his gun and struck him to the ground. Could this be true, monsieur?'

'It's true.'

Frénaye gazed for a moment, then shuddered. 'My soul, and you are still alive! But that was the turning point, monsieur. Now, by her own witness, she could confirm that Cartier's act was not condoned by you. Everything I could tell her was confirmation, and we talked of you, monsieur, by the hour. Only, alas, she was now in despair at the thought of those times when she had betrayed you.'

'She was never to blame.'

'Oh monsieur, she is proud! She cannot bear the shame of having been so credulous. Twice, three times she was made the instrument to set you up as a target for Starnberg. To understand this was deep bitterness to her and she could not speak of it without tears. Monsieur, there must be time for these wounds to heal. Her pride as yet will not let her face you.'

'But ... something I must do!'

'You must trust her, monsieur.'

'Frénaye, for a month I've been living in hell.'

'Monsieur, you must live there a little longer, and trust mademoiselle. There is no remedy.'

No remedy! Yet somewhere out there, within miles, she could be waiting too: had perhaps come, if come she had, not entirely on the account of the worthless Hénault ... Set them together face to face, and could the miracle fail to happen: would not pride, shame, suffering itself dissolve and vanish in that moment?

'Meanwhile, monsieur,' Frénaye began. 'With regard to the misfortunes of Monsieur Barentin—'

A tap at the door interrupted him; it opened to reveal Empton.

'Don't get up, old man,' Empton said. 'Just ask me to join the party.'

But he was already in the room and easing shut the door behind him. He eyed Frénaye with a tigerish smile, then went to help himself from Gently's bottle. He was wearing a figure-hugging silk dressing gown that exposed a tanned, hairy chest.

'Slainte. Aren't you going to introduce me?'

'Monsieur Frénaye,' Gently grunted.

'Ah?' Empton said.

'He's also a guest here. Monsieur speaks only French.'

'Ah yes, the French connection,' Empton said. 'One relies on you to pick up Frogs.' Then to Frénaye in French: 'Enchanted, monsieur. Do let me top up your glass.'

'Monsieur —?'

'Your glass, monsieur.'

He advanced the bottle towards Frénaye; then, with a bright smile, poured whisky in a stream into Frénaye's lap.

'*Mais non—mais non —!*' Frénaye sprang up.

'Just checking, old man,' Empton leered at Gently. 'In fact, I've dropped in for a couple of words, not necessarily for publication.' To Frénaye he said: 'So sorry, monsieur. But whisky does wonders for the nap.'

Frénaye glared and patted himself with his handkerchief. Empton took a seat on Gently's bed. Deliberately, Gently turned his shoulder, slowly refilled and lit his pipe. Empton sipped.

'Your attention, old man.'

Gently blew smoke at the ceiling.

'I've been reconsidering your offer, old man, wondering whether it wouldn't fit in somewhere.'

'So,' Gently said.

'I think perhaps it might, knowing the heroic stances you favour. Also the Frogs would love it – just imagine the impression on wet legs here. Of course it depends on how the situation develops, whether some sort of stalemate emerges. I'm hoping it doesn't, but if it does your little gambit might be the key to it.'

Gently turned to stare. 'Go on,' he said.

'Consider cases,' Empton said. 'We find them, we bottle them up, then the Frogs get cold feet. So then we want a legitimate move to restore fluidity to the situation.'

'In other words, to start the shooting.'

'Naughty,' Empton said. 'But about right. Exchange situations are tense, little rushes of blood do sometimes occur.'

'No.' Gently said.

Empton clicked his tongue. 'Don't rush to decisions, old man,' he said. 'You aren't reading the small print. This way our Yiddisher friend stands a snowball's chance of walking out. To a point, I think I can control my nervousness in the presence of the ungodly. My promise that he gets clear before excitement takes over.'

'More likely he'll be caught in crossfire.'

'So that's a chance,' Empton said. 'But leave him there and no chance – he's booked for an interview with Father Abraham.'

'I'll do it, but on my terms.'

'Ah, these sentimentalists,' Empton said. 'If you do it on any terms, old man, your neck will be stuck out to infinity. So what's it to you? I take it you can bear to see the ungodly laid to rest.'

'My terms or none.'

'Well, well,' Empton said. 'Who says the Boy's Own Paper is dead?' He smiled winningly. 'Very well, old man, what ho and all that.'

'My terms are that Guthrie is in control.'

Empton sipped. His eyes were small. 'Not so naive then, are we, old man?'

'Not so naive,' Gently said.

'Ah,' Empton said. 'Ah. Hero having second thoughts. I thought you were quick off the mark, old man, with your offer to exchange necks.'

Gently said nothing.

Empton finished his drink. Suddenly, he jerked the glass through the open window. One heard its faint shatter on the pavement below. Empton showed his teeth.

'Well, thank you, old man. Just thought I'd drop round for the chat. Enjoy your stay.'

Gently said nothing.

Empton sighed, rose and left.

The door closed, and another slammed a few steps down the corridor. Then there was silence for a while, the only interruption a car's horn hooting. At last Frénaye glanced timidly at Gently.

'Monsieur, I do understand a little English ...'

Gently hunched, knocked out his pipe. He poured another finger, draining the bottle.

'That man is your Empton ...?'

'That's him.'

'Alas! Poor Monsieur Barentin. Monsieur, I told you that Cartier frightened me, but compared with this man he is a child.' Frénaye hesitated. 'Can it be true that you have offered yourself as exchange hostage?'

'After Starnberg, it might tempt them.'

'But monsieur, it is complete madness.' Frénaye gazed in distress. 'They will agree, but only to shoot you. They will never give up Monsieur Barentin. No, no, monsieur, do not think of it, there must be other ways yet to try. This Empton knows it cannot succeed, he wishes only to use you to begin a slaughter.'

'Guthrie will prevent it.'

'Still, they will shoot you, you will be killed for no purpose whatever.'

'At the moment I can think of no better alternative.'

'Then, monsieur, you must be in love with death.'

Gently drank. Frénaye chewed on his pipe. In the room was the stink of spilled whisky. The Frenchman was holding his face averted, keeping his eyes to himself.

'Listen monsieur ... if we could get to them first, might there not be a way then?'

'Can we get to them first?'

'I have indeed information which, it is possible, may lead us to them. Then, when we have reconnoitred, some plan of action may occur to us. This at least will have greater purpose than the useless sacrifice you are contemplating.'

Gently was silent a moment. Finally he said:

'What have you got?'

'Monsieur, this will go no further ...'

'It won't go to Monsieur Empton.'

'Then it is this. The area we are seeking is in the neighbourhood of Invergarry, where they are holding Monsieur Barentin in a remote and deserted house. Of the location of the latter I know only that it is near an old road to Skye.'

'To Skye!'

'Does monsieur know it?'

Gently shook his head and reached for the phone. After an interval a porter knocked to deliver a dusty map.

'This is all we have, sir —'

'Wait,' Gently said. 'What do you know of old roads to Skye?'

The man looked blank. 'They're all old, sir. I have not heard tell of a new one.'

'Perhaps a road that has been abandoned?'

'Ach, I think I'm with you now! After the war they built a fine new highway between Invergarry and Lochalsh. The old road went by way of Glengarry, but it will be in a sad state now.'

'Show me.'

They pored over the map. The porter traced the road up Glengarry. Hatched lines departed at Tomdoun and wriggled their way north through close packed contours. Causeways carried them across two lochs, but marked habitations there were none. At Tomdoun, a phone box. Across the mountains, Cluanie Lodge.

'Thank you.'

The porter departed. They remained staring at the swirls of the map. A far country indeed: even along Glengarry marked houses were few and distant from each other. From Kinloch-hourn, at the head of the glen, the road faded to a track departing into Knoydart.

'Monsieur', Frénaye said, 'can obtain guns?'

'Possibly one gun,' Gently said.

'He has transport?'

'He has.'

'Then, tomorrow ...?'

'What have we to lose?' He gave Frénaye a hard stare. 'We could perhaps lunch at Invergarry.'

Frénaye avoided his eye. 'Possibly a packed lunch ...?'

Gently said nothing; went to close the window.

'The police have gone back down the glen,' he'd told the bearded man. 'With the glasses I could see them plainly. They parked by the phone box, two men with a van. While one made a call, the other exercised a dog.'

'Jesus,' the bearded man had said. 'Did they have a dog?'

'Yes monsieur, I think an Alsatian. It was off the leash for several minutes, running this way and that. Then the man came out of the box and he and the second man had a conversation. They looked once or twice in this direction, but then whistled the dog and drove off down the glen.'

'They didn't catch sight of you, Frenchie?'

'Monsieur, I have played these games before.'

'Aye, you're a useful lad, Frenchie,' the bearded man had said. 'I'm thinking you'll have earned that stake in Aden. Will you be for South America?'

'I think so monsieur. I have friends and contacts in Rio.'

'A fine place, Frenchie, when you're flush – no lack of *senoritas* there!' The bearded man had patted his shoulder. 'But I don't like to hear of the dog.'

'Monsieur, they are satisfied. They have gone.'

'Maybe, maybe,' he'd said. 'Ach, well! Get in and relieve Dusty, who is itching to stretch his legs. And Frenchie.'

'Monsieur?'

'Keep your mouth shut, comprenez? I don't want you gabbing to the old Jew.'

4

But after all it wasn't going to be so easy to slink off unnoticed on a private venture. By morning the affair had taken a fresh turn, with Gently catapulted back to stage centre. At breakfast Empton slammed down a Scotsman by Gently's plate.

'This is what they call press cooperation!'

With as much pedal as *The Scotsman* ever permitted itself, the story had been spread across the front page:

MYSTERY POLICE SEARCH IN INVERNESS-SHIRE
'Tight Security' comment
Connection With Wrecked Plane Riddle
Top Yard Man's Presence 'Coincidental'

And there was a picture of a smiling Gently over a caption loaded with innuendo; it hadn't escaped *The Scotsman's* attention that he had recently been involved with French Security.

'Guthrie's called a Press Conference,' Empton said. 'You'll have to play it tighter than tight, old man. I've rung London, and they'll confirm any tale you care to tell about swopping observers. And just remember it's dynamite. The French story is that Barentin's cruising in the Med.'

'What is Guthrie going to tell them?' Gently said.

'Ah,' Empton said. 'I like the *cannabis* angle. About half a ton makes good reading. Everyone's conditioned to half tons of *cannabis*.'

'You'll be letting him in for it.'

'I'm crying old man. His job is to keep them off my back.'

From a single table in the corner of the dining room Frénaye observed them with mournful eyes.

At the police station Guthrie was in a sweat; he was on the phone explaining to someone. People were dashing in and out of the office and a pile of paper was mounting on his desk.

'That bastard, that sod Empton—!'

Red-faced, he grabbed Gently's arm. But then the phone went again immediately and he was snarling instructions to someone at Beauly.

'Listen! Apart from all the lies I've got to tell there's this bloody Frenchman called Gautier – an honorary consul or some damned thing – rings up and wants to talk to Mossoo Gently.'

'I'll handle him,' Gently said.

'It's a bloody nightmare. Who's going to believe this crud about *cannabis*? You've seen the paper. If I mention *cannabis* they'll laugh like a hundred drains.'

'Say illicit cargo. Let them jump to conclusions.'

'The trouble is I'm a godawful liar. And as if that wasn't enough he's making this an excuse to step up the hunt still further.'

When he'd cooled off, Gently mentioned the gun, and Guthrie stared meanly for a moment. Then, without a word, he sat down and dashed off a requisition.

'Take this to Tate. But ... off the record?'

'Let's say I've got a hunch. From studying the map.'

Guthrie shook his head. 'That's more than I have! You don't want to tell me?'

'Not at this stage.'

About to let it go, Guthrie added: 'For chrissake don't go sticking your neck out. Leave it to the man – if he stops a bullet, you and I can laugh all the way to the mortuary.'

The press conference was timed for ten-thirty and there the questions came fast and curvy. Besides *The Scotsman* half-a-dozen nationals, three locals and the BBC had sent representatives. Flashlights fizzed: empty-eyed men prodded and wheedled the unhappy Guthrie, got to the *cannabis* in no time flat, set him quivering with adroit insinuations. Then it was Gently's turn:

'Is this a one-off, Chiefie?'

'London will give you full details.'

'But why Inverness?'

'Its problems are typical of policing in a scattered area.'

'Chiefie, how much of a coincidence is a coincidence?'

'Every four minutes a crime is committed ...'

Nobody was believing anybody: you might have cut the incredulity with a rusty dirk. But it was the Frenchman, Gautier, an oil-company executive, who had his finger closest to the pulse. Meeting Gently later in Guthrie's office, he said:

'Monsieur, a contact in the Quai D'Orsay informs me ...'

Did he really know what was afoot? A short, stout man with five o'clock shadow, he mingled compliments with knowing assertions. After dead-batting him for twenty minutes Gently was still uncertain how they stood; then the Frenchman reached into a bag he had with him and produced a magnum of champagne:

'A tribute from the Minister ...'

It appeared that he actually did hold an official position!

Time wasted: before he could get away it was nearly noon. He found Frénaye fretting in hotel reception with a picnic basket beside him.

'Monsieur has the guns?'

'One gun.'

It was a standard service revolver: its muzzle velocity about one third that of a Czech M52.

They unravelled Inverness's tiresome one-way and struck the Dores road from town. Suburbs gave way to wooded country and then to the old military road along the loch shore. The day was misty; Ness, a pale panel drowning the reflections of purplish hills. Broken wake-lines suggested mysteries by their illusory motion down the loch. On the far shore uneasy traffic showed through gaps in screens of trees; on their own side traffic was light, though cars were parked on a succession of laybys.

'Monsieur ...'

Frénaye broke a silence apparently devoted to a study of the scenery. Dressed today in a neat-fitting windcheater, he looked every centimetre an earnest tourist.

'If I dare to speak it ... while monsieur was absent, I took the opportunity to make a phone call. Merely to confirm, it is understood, that the situation persists as reported.'

'And?' Gently said.

'That is all, monsieur. There have been no developments. But I made use of the occasion to pass on the intelligence with which monsieur surprised me last night.'

'Thanks,' Gently growled.

Frénaye stared ahead. 'I must stress, monsieur, there have been no developments. Our mission remains a reconnaissance on the information in hand.'

Tight mouthed, Gently drove on. In other words, she still wouldn't see him! For a moment the knowledge stung him, filled him with a bitterness of despair. Had she ceased to love him ...? Thrusting into his mind came images pre-dating the nightmare in the forest: if they were as valid for her as for him, how could they fail to bridge this crevasse? Trust her, Frénaye had said. Yet, if she loved him, would there not have been a word, a sign ...?

They climbed through Foyers and were diverted into the rugged country behind the loch. At last the road emerged high above Fort Augustus, a small, white town beside a stairway of locks. Here mountains heaped upon the Great Glen, which seemed to lose its way in the misty confusion; below, the toe-end of Ness lay clear and reflecting, contained by a dark, hard shoreline.

'Monsieur, I have been considering tactics,' Frénaye said as they freewheeled down to the town. 'At some point, it is certain, we must leave the car and proceed on foot.'

'So,' Gently grunted.

'It will be an advantage, monsieur, if we assume an appearance of innocence. If, like many I see, we equip ourselves with rucksacks, peaked caps and rolled impermeables.'

Gently shrugged, but the idea was sound. They parked in Fort Augustus and sought a sports shop. Along with the gear suggested by Frénaye he bought also a drab anorak, two OS maps and a cheap pair of glasses. Frénaye hovered over an air pistol, rejecting it finally with a sigh. Then, impatient at the fresh delay, Gently hustled them back to the car.

'But we shall not regret the impermeables, monsieur ...'

The mist was turning to rain. With wipers sweeping they hissed along the level road to Invergarry. A modest village, it marked the junction of the Great Glen road with the road to Skye: a few houses, a filling station, a ruined castle ... and a hotel. Involuntarily, Gently eased the car. His eyes devoured the hotel. It stood back from the road, white walled, slate roofed, almost opposite a layby carved deep under trees. A wall concealed its car park so that only the roofs of cars were visible ...

Straight in front of him stared Frénaye, his neat face inscrutable. But he knew: he knew! It was there if anywhere, behind those white walls ... the aloof windows ...

Round a bend, at the end of the village, stood a post office store with parking beside it. Gently flashed, pulled over, drove into the parking and cut his engine.

'Monsieur …?'

Frénaye's eyes were wary.

'How many shops can there be in Glengarry?'

'While that is true, monsieur … would not one suppose that, already …?'

'So we'll check it again.'

He dived out through the rain. Frénaye followed reluctantly. The long, cluttered store had just then few customers and a woman sat disengaged at the post office counter. Gently showed his warrant.

'Police. I'm enquiring about three men.'

The woman looked surprised. 'But Sergeant McBain was in here yesterday about them.'

'A Frenchman, a bearded Scot and an Arab. Only one may have come into the shop.'

'That's just certain,' the woman said. 'But as I told the sergeant, we have foreigners in and out here all the time.'

'Were you shown pictures?'

She wasn't; Gently produced the photostats. The woman peered at them with interest, hesitating at last over that of Hénault.

'Would that be the Frenchman?'

'Do you recognise him?'

'I would not quite be certain,' she said. 'But if he had shaved off his moustache he might be the man who came in Tuesday morning.'

'Go on,' Gently said.

'Well, he came in early, almost as soon as I opened the door. He brought a list of groceries with him − I doubt if he spoke three words of English.'

'Was there a car?'

'There was. A dark coloured car is all I can tell you.'

'Passengers?'

'I could not say.'

'Which way was it heading?'

'Ach … Lochalsh way, I'm thinking.'

'And he made a phone call, this man?'

'Have you second sight, then!' the woman said. 'Aye, now I come to think of it he was in the booth while I was getting his order. I did not pay much attention, the phone is there for bodies to use ... wait! I remember this. He wrote something down, perhaps a number from the book.'

'How long was he here?'

'Just about ten minutes. The time it took me to put up his bits.'

Gently crossed to the booth. The phone was STD. He flipped through the code book lying on the shelf. He found the Rouen code: beside it was a faint mark made by a ball pen. He consulted the local directory for the entry for the Invergarry Hotel. Here there was no mark, but a ghost of an indentation on the margin.

'Did the man ask any questions?'

'Nothing at all. But can you not tell me why he is wanted?'

'Thank you for your help,' Gently said. 'If he turns up again, please give us a ring.'

'Ach!' the woman said disgustedly. 'But wait – wait. Is there word yet of Constable Dickie?'

'Dickie?'

'Our local policeman. According to the sergeant, he's gone missing.'

Hand on door, Gently checked. 'How long has he been missed?'

'Oh, just this morning. He and the sergeant were searching the glen yesterday. Today they were to search Glen Roy, but Dickie didn't turn up at the rendezvous. The sergeant couldn't raise him on the phone, so he rang us to hear if we'd seen him.'

'You hadn't.'

'No. Nor he's not at his lodging. Nor his van nor his dog neither. They were to have met down at Spean Bridge, and I'm just hoping there has not been an accident.'

'If I hear of him I'll let you know.'

'Aye, it will be kind,' the woman said. 'We are special friends, not to mention cousins. It would grieve me to hear he had taken harm.'

The rain now was sheeting down, hiding the strath and the hills beyond. Back in the car, Gently mopped his face and turned an unrelenting stare on Frénaye.

'Shall we have it on the table, monsieur?'

'I do not comprehend—' Frénaye began.

'Monsieur, you comprehend very well, and you shall hear me spell it out to you step by step. On Tuesday morning the kidnappers stopped here and Hénault was sent in to buy stores.

Hénault rang a number in Rouen with an SOS, a request doubtless for a car, money and a false passport. But how next to get in touch with his contact? He remembers the hotel down the road. He instructs his contact to take up quarters there and wait till he can call again. His contact rings you, then follows the instructions. Subsequently the second call comes. Thus the contact, and in due course yourself, know roughly where the kidnappers are hiding. And at this very moment, a few yards from this spot, the contact sits waiting for the call that matters. Back there, monsieur, in the hotel. Where, in two minutes, we could be with her ...'

For some time Frénaye stared at the rain that coursed busily down the windscreen, hands buried in pockets, head sunk in the collar of the windcheater. At last his shoulders heaved in a sigh.

'No, monsieur,' he said. 'No. Monsieur is shrewd but monsieur is impetuous. It may also be that, in his impatience, monsieur is being led astray by his wishes. Monsieur, I have never identified my source. There monsieur jumped at once to a conclusion. He has not considered that the source might be criminal and so highly sensitive with regard to identity.'

Gently gazed. 'Are you telling me—!'

'Nothing, monsieur. I tell you nothing. Except perhaps that, if I may venture an opinion, we need fear no indiscretion from the source in question. And meanwhile, monsieur, we have business ahead which may take all our time until night.'

Gently gave him an incredulous look, then started the engine and backed off the parking. The wipers clucked as they shouldered the rain. Frénaye's face was as blank as a Buddha's.

Three miles later they reached the junction of the road that wound its way up the length of Glengarry. A single-track ribbon, it dropped down from the Skye road to follow the shore of the first of three lochs. Across the water Ben Tee and neighbouring peaks made fitful appearances through the wrack; on their own side steep, tree-clad slopes rose high to lose themselves in murk. They met no traffic. The bumpy little road twisted, turned, rose and fell, threading through glades of oak and ash, opening views of dark moorland. It was a road that doubled each mile. Only twice did they pass habitations. Meanwhile the loch narrowed, and sometimes ahead one glimpsed the fan of peaks guarding far Loch Hourn. Finally, with the rain easing, they passed the small hotel of

Tomdoun, followed by ruined walls among trees, an isolated phone box: and a lane-like turn off.

'Here ...'

Frénaye had a map open. Gently braked, ran the car under trees. Unless on the alert one would have passed that forlorn junction, which nevertheless had once been the main road to Skye. A lonely spot: the hotel, out of sight, was the single habitation in that part of the glen. Behind them stretched empty, high moors, before the River Garry and roadless hills. And there the phone box, opposite the junction ... in all the long glen: one!

'We'll eat.'

Frénaye looked relieved. He hoisted up the basket and unpacked their picnic. In fact, it was worth delaying until the fading rain returned again to mist. The portals of Hourn, through which the wrack had been streaming, now were drawn hard on a greenish sky: the Atlantic was relenting. And, while they ate, that red-painted box stayed under their eyes ...

'My guess is they're not far away.'

'Monsieur has spoken my thoughts,' Frénaye said. 'A telephone is essential to their plans, and they would prefer to approach it without use of a car.'

'There is also this.' Gently pointed to the map. 'Within three miles the road reaches Loch Loyne. The crossing was presumably by means of a causeway, and the odds are that by now it is no longer usable.'

'Then, my dear colleague, the less ground to cover.'

'For one of us,' Gently said, 'no ground at all. One man will be less conspicuous than two – and I'm the man who is carrying a gun.'

'But, monsieur!' Frénaye expostulated.

'Monsieur, I desire an eye to be kept on the phone box. I may or may not discover the hideout, but that phone box is a certain point of contact.'

Frénaye looked sulky. 'Monsieur is disagreeable. It was understood that we ventured together.'

'Monsieur, today is strictly a reconnaissance, as you were kind enough to remind me earlier.'

The rain ceased. Gently donned the anorak and packed his jacket into the rucksack. He attached the 'impermeable', pulled on the cap, slung the glasses by his side and shouldered his load.

'Give me three hours.'

'And then, monsieur ...?'

'After three hours consult your initiative.'

He stalked away under the trees without looking back at the resentful Frénaye.

'Warning: weakened bridges – unsafe for traffic'. The sign was an old one with flaking paint. But the first long stretch of crumbling tarmac strode tamely enough across the rain-darkened moors. On the left a deer fence protected young pine saplings, on the right rocky knolls humped above the heather; then there were islands of trees, level plashes of water, and ahead denser trees and the long spur of a low hill. One saw cotton grass, harebells, orchids, the yellow stars of tormentil beside the track; and circling the horizon a theatre of peaks, blued and sharpening in dissolving mist.

But there was no sign of habitation in that unruly, abandoned landscape. No sheep grazed there, or cattle; no sheltering grey wall capped any of the knolls. Only the road had gone that way, crossing country that none had ventured to settle: from lonely Tomdoun to lonely Cluanie. And now the road itself a ghost ...

So, how good was Frénaye's information? After the first half mile it seemed, very little. The broken, grass-grown road offered few suggestions of recent traffic. Scanning it as he marched along, Gently could spot no tell-tale oilstains, rubber smear or fresh crumblings of the weather-picked surface. It wasn't proof, but it was discouraging. And meanwhile the country grew wilder, emptier. Reaching the dense stand of trees, he halted to survey the scene with glasses.

At this point the road had begun to climb and provided a useful viewpoint. Far off, in the direction of Tomdoun, he could still see the red spot of the phone box. Followed the broken expanse of moor, knolls, pools, groups of trees, and finally the long scarp of the hill that closed the landscape to the north. And then something that brought back his glasses with a jerk! A faint line of track was visible on the moor; reaching out from the trees behind him, it proceeded to a knoll clothed in tall sycamores. He focused on the knoll. He could see only trees. Yet the track ended there, didn't resume beyond. An island site offering cover enough: perhaps a third of a mile from where he stood ...

He jammed the glasses back in their case and hastened on into the trees. Within a hundred yards he came to the junction of the track with the road. Originally of granite chip, it was now bound hard and choked with grass: but where it joined the road a skim of mud showed the unmistakable imprint of a tyre. He went down the track; at the edge of the trees he again focused glasses on the knoll. Still nothing to see: just the track, swinging round to vanish behind the sycamores.

What to do now!

For several minutes he studied the knoll and its surroundings, but clearly a nearer approach from that direction was ruled out. The track was bare of cover and must be regarded as under observation; furthermore a lookout, if there was one, would have had him in view all the way from Tomdoun. He would have been seen to enter the trees: now, without too much delay, he must be seen to leave them ... it was also probable that, from higher up the road, a more revealing view might be had of the knoll.

He regained the road. It continued to climb until clear of the belt of trees but then, exasperatingly, bore left, keeping the trees between him and the knoll. Sweating, he toiled along between verges lined with meadow-sweet and foxglove, always with the deer fence to his left, the birch-scattered moorland to his right. At last, after much meandering, the road crested a slight rise, bringing into view what was apparently Loch Loyne and the dishevelled blocks of its former causeway. A judgement confirmed ... but the knoll with the sycamores? He left the road and struggled through heather. A hundred yards distant, fenced with scrub birches, a platform of rock made a convenient eminence. He climbed up through twigs, through bracken, and focused the glasses. He could see a house!

A house: a low, stone-walled cottage, with small, blank windows and slated roof: about a mile away, set close to the sycamores, and invisible from any viewpoint but this. A half-ruined house: he could see gaps where slates had shed from rafters: probably abandoned when the new road was opened, forgotten, erased from their maps by cartographers ...

For twenty minutes he watched it, seeing in that time not a flicker of movement. If there was a car it was out of sight, parked either in the trees or behind the cottage. But that this was the hideout he could have no doubt: it was the only habitation south of the causeway. Invisible, unsuspected, almost unapproachable, it was a perfect choice for McGash's purpose. To effect a rescue ... how was it possible? A car would be spotted from far away. By night as well as by day they would have a watcher: and a gun always pointed at Barentin's head.

But a closer look ... that might be possible! Grunting, Gently put away the glasses. It meant some heavy going through the rough, but ... keeping to the clumps, the rocky outcrops ...

In effect it was easier than he had suppose: he struck a burn that drained southwards towards the Garry. Shuffling, often sodden-footed, along its course, he drew closer and closer to the knoll of the sycamores. At quarter of a mile's distance he halted to observe, lying prone in wet bracken. Now, with the glasses, he could study detail, spot movement, if any, at the deep-set windows. But still ... nothing stirred! So where was their lookout? Did they feel so secure that they hadn't set one? His eye passed, returned to the shadowed porch: a darker shadow showed the door to be ajar.

He crept on along his comfortless gully. No challenge, no alarm came from the cottage. All he could hear was the chuckle of the burn and the chinking of a stonechat somewhere above. He was close: too close. Squirming flat to the heather, he made a gap to observe again. Yes ... the door was ajar: and there was something else: a few yards from the door lay the body of a dog ...

He drew his gun. Nothing moved. He rose, ran crouching to flatten himself against the cottage wall. The dog was an Alsatian. Its head was blown off. The body lay stiffened and sodden with rain. Gun-first, he kicked the door wide. Sprawled inside was the body of a man. A policeman, he lay clutching his stomach with bloody hands, his mouth in a snarl, his eyes staring. Gently went by him. The cottage was deserted. Sleeping bags, clutter, lay about the rooms. In the kitchen, a carton containing groceries, a camping stove, tins.

He left. He set himself a trot, panted back to the road, pounded on towards the phone box. It seemed never to grow bigger. While it was still some way off he saw a car pass it: a green Deux-Chevaux.

Lounging in one of the comfortable chairs, the bearded man sipped from a glass. Sitting like that he looked almost amiable, relaxed, half amused. But then you noticed, protruding from an armpit, the handle of the gun he wore night and day. He was an educated man, the Frenchman had decided, in spite of his trick of using the vernacular. At moments of stress, when giving orders, the lilt vanished from his speech.

'So now you know the truth of it, Frenchie,' he said. 'I wasn't kittling you up about Dusty. I mean, shooting a policeman, that's venial, but to blow away his poor doggie! Aye, I'm afraid he has a nasty nature. You can never teach a wog to be kind to brutes.'

'But he had no option, Jamie,' the Frenchman said. 'You or I would have done the same.'

'Would you now,' the bearded man said. 'That's interesting, Frenchie, very interesting.' He drank. 'But what do you think of our quarters – isn't this better than a shift up the glen?'

'Oh yes, Jamie,' the Frenchman said. 'Yet I am wondering ... is it wise?'

'Is it wise!' The bearded man laughed. 'It's just the canniest move in the book. They'll not be back searching here again – for one thing, they haven't the men to spare for it. No, no, we shall sit tight here till the caper is over and the cash paid – and the cash is on its way, Frenchie. That's the word I had from Glasgow.'

'And our comrades, Jamie?'

The bearded man drank. 'That's a different story,' he said. 'I'm thinking there are words to put to that bargain – they'll not trust us over-much concerning Abraham. But cash, they're always free with that, and a plane you can have for the asking. So drink up, Frenchie man – your part of the deal is cut and dried.'

The Frenchman drank. 'You're a remarkable man, Jamie.'

'Aye, some would say so,' the bearded man said. 'And Frenchie – feel free to kick the furniture. This joint is costing us a hundred a week.'

5

Guthrie put down the office phone; he kept his face turned from Gently. 'They've found his van,' he said. 'He left it parked behind the shielings under the trees. No doubt he thought the walk would exercise the dog.' He leaned hard against the desk. 'The poor laddie.'

Tate said: 'He was twenty-six, sir. He was engaged to the daughter of the people at the store.'

'And they shot him down.' Guthrie made his fingers creak. 'My God and soul we'll get those devils. Put me in sight of them. That's all I ask.'

'He mentioned the cottage to McBain yesterday,' Tate said. 'They stopped at the box to phone in. But McBain thought it too unlikely and they carried on down.'

'Unlikely, unlikely,' Guthrie said. 'Who could have guessed they would know such a place. And the laddie goes back there in his own time to make sure – just to make sure! He'd have walked in there like a lamb, Tate. Told the dog to sit. Then walked in.'

'Rotten luck, sir,' Tate said.

Guthrie clenched his fists and sat silent

Empton came in; he glanced around.

'Well, well,' he said. 'Well, well.'

He closed the door, pulled up a chair to the desk and sat.

'Information,' he said. 'If you want a name I can give you one, Yousef Hajjar. A typical job, two bullets. He's what you might call a ballistics expert.'

Guthrie stared at him.

'Ah,' Empton said. 'Well, a round up of the rest of the news. We've McGash's and Hajjar's dabs plus two other sets, doubtless Hénault's and Barentin's. So Barentin is still alive, or was still alive, allowing for any moments of natural impatience. Under drugs I rather fancy, since we found an empty paraldehyde bottle. Then there are these.' He produced two expended shells. 'Skoda of course, but that's academic.'

'Listen,' Guthrie said. 'Where are they now?'

'Tut,' Empton said. 'Such impatience. Wonderful what a dead wollie can do in getting enthusiastic cooperation. Perhaps we're beginning to see eye-to-eye.'

Guthrie struck the desk. 'I want those men.'

'Of course old man,' Empton said. 'At the end of a gun. Isn't that the meaning of the glitter in your eye?'

Guthrie looked away. Empton laughed.

'Give your conscience a rest old man,' he said. 'We're way beyond morals. Terrorism negates them. We're operating in conditions of total pragmatism.'

'I want them in a cell,' Guthrie said.

'You want them dead.'

'I want them put away for good and all.'

'Not you,' Empton said. 'Not you. You want to see them holding their guts like your wollie. You want revenge, I want a solution. That puts us in the same boat. The difference is that I keep my poise while you're knocked off balance by your emotions.'

Guthrie's hands jerked. 'Just let's get them.'

Empton laughed again. 'So hear now,' he said. 'While your wollie was flushing them out of the glen, my men were severing their hot line to Paris.'

'Doing what,' Guthrie said.

'Nobbling their agent. We do have our moments,' Empton said. 'A jock called Petrie, better known in Glasgow as a car-ringer and fixer. We've had an eye on him for some while on account of his colourful acquaintants. I had his phone tapped. He rang a certain Paris number, very naughty. So we closed him down.'

'You mean you've arrested him?'

'Something like that. The Frogs meanwhile will have copped his contact. It was a toss up whether to let them rip, old man, but on balance I felt this way would be quickest. You see Petrie will know where McGash has gone. And Petrie will be delivered here shortly.'

Guthrie's eyes were small. 'But ... will he talk?'

Empton showed his teeth. 'I shouldn't wonder old man. But while we're waiting there's another matter which has been puzzling my naive mind.' He turned for the first time to Gently, who was sitting apart by the window. 'Your luck, old man, your proverbial luck. I know it's damned bad form to question it. But do tell us how, with all of Scotland to choose from, you happened first time on the very spot.'

Gently remained staring through the window. 'I applied your appraisal to a map,' he said at last.

'Oh come on,' Empton said. 'You're among friends. Be British and all that.'

'Glengarry seemed a probable area. The phone box suggested a point of departure.'

'And from there – straight to it?'

'I explored the road, saw the cottage and investigated.'

'Oh brilliant,' Empton said. 'A man with X-ray eyes. He sees through trees and solid rock.'

'I saw the track and made a detour until I could see to where it led.'

'And then, because no one shot at you, you walked straight in and found the wollie.'

'Something like that,' Gently said.

'You're lovely,' Empton said. 'Oh you're lovely.' He made nickering sounds with his tongue. 'All the same, I keep getting this feeling that men are at work somewhere. Then I ask myself, why would Lucky Jim take a Froggy new chum up the glen with him?'

'Frénaye is a police officer,' Gently said.

'Nice,' Empton said. 'Do tell us some more. Like how he turns up in a hotel bedroom just before your blinding success with a dead wollie.'

Gently said: 'He's here unofficially.'

'But he's here,' Empton said. 'Here.'

'Frénaye was involved in the original police hunt. He is also acquainted with Monsieur Barentin.'

'And,' Empton said.

Gently was silent.

'I think I ought to know about this,' Guthrie said. 'Official or unofficial, I think I should know what a French policeman is doing on my patch.'

'Let me guess,' Empton said to the ceiling. 'Barentin was snatched near Deauville-Trouville. If our Frog was involved in the police hunt then he must be stationed in that area. So Lucky Jim knows him, he knows Lucky Jim. And suddenly we find him at Lucky Jim's side. And straight-way Lucky Jim puts his finger on the hideout which every damned policeman in Scotland has been searching for. My oh my, what a coincidence. Surely one for the Book of Records.'

Guthrie turned to stare at Gently. 'Was it like that?'

'Let me guess a little more,' Empton said. 'Lucky Jim knows Hénault's ex-wife, in fact I seem to recall he knows her rather well. And she would know the Frog – how it all fits together! – and before her Hénault might not be discreet. So some information trickles through that is much too stalky for Lucky Jim to lay on the table.' Empton showed his teeth. 'You've been naughty old man. And it's cost our friend a wollie.'

Gently said levelly: 'I had no information that could have prevented the death of Constable Dickie.'

'But,' Empton said, 'you had information.'

Gently ignored him, spoke to Guthrie. 'Frénaye is here on his own initiative because of his concern for Monsieur Barentin. In addition he learned from the Yard that I was engaged on the case.'

'Oh how convenient,' Empton said, 'And almost true.'

'It is true I am engaged on this case.'

'Ha, ha,' Empton said. 'And that gives you the right to sit on vital information.'

'Was there information?' Guthrie said.

'A very small pointer,' Gently said. 'Given to me personally on the understanding that it would not be used to Monsieur Barentin's peril. In my judgement, that might have been the case if the information was prematurely revealed.'

'Now,' Empton said, 'I've heard everything. In other words you weren't to tell me.'

'In other words,' Gently said.

Empton picked up a ball pen from the desk and snapped it.

'Old man,' he said. 'Get this very straight. This show is outside your moral parameters and I won't take interference from God himself. So you love Jews, you love Frenchmen, you're the hair on Jesus' chin. But I'm the bastard they bring in when the other bastards have shot the umpire. That's my job and I know my job. And heaven help you if you cross me.'

Gently turned to stare at Empton.

'Now old man – that information.'

Gently took out his pipe and slowly began to fill it.

'Is there—is there anything fresh, man?' Guthrie faltered.

Gently lit the pipe, shrugged. 'My information related to the cottage. Unfortunately it came too late.'

'You've nothing that could help us now.'

'Nothing.'

After a moment Empton showed his teeth. 'Well, well,' he said. 'So after all there wasn't much to be coy about, old man. Of course it might be useful to know the source.' His chill eye rested briefly on Gently's. 'But doubtless all that's academic. And in the meantime we do have Petrie.'

Gently puffed.

'Yes, Petrie,' Empton said.

'What charge are you holding him on?' Guthrie asked.

'Oh nothing special,' Empton said. 'In fact none at all. I believe he expressed a wish to make himself helpful.'

It was past ten when a car parked in the yard and a man was hustled up to Guthrie's office. In charge of two blank-faced Special Branch men, he looked dazed and staggered when pushed towards a chair. About thirty-three or four, he had fleshy features, greasy fair hair, big, clumsy hands. He was sweating; he had a bruise on his jaw. When he sat down he did so wincing.

'And has he been a good boy?' Empton said to the men.

'He's a good boy now, Chief,' one of them said. 'Cooperative, I think you'll find him.'

'That's the name of the game,' Empton said.

He drew out the gold cigarette case, lit a straw-coloured cigarette and inhaled several times. He lounged against the desk, crossing his legs. He gazed down on the prisoner almost tenderly.

'Ah, Petrie,' he said.

Petrie shrank on the chair. He was smelling of fear. Empton blew smoke in his face.

'Petrie,' he said. 'You're in trouble I think.'

'Petrie coughed and rubbed his eyes. Empton blew more smoke in his face. Petrie tried to duck away from it. One of the men held him straight in the chair. Empton blew more smoke.

'Listen Petrie,' he said. 'This is the way of it. I shan't bother to put you away, that would be a waste of taxpayer's money. Instead I'll drop word that you were bought and leave the opposition to make arrangements.' He blew smoke. 'I'm like that,' he said. 'Always an eye to the public funds.'

'But I haven't done nothing—!' Petrie gasped.

Empton clicked his tongue. 'My dear old chap. We have it on tape, we have it on film. Don't waste my time with comic remarks.'

'But I tell you I haven't!'

Empton inhaled a deep lungful and sprayed it steadily at the coughing Petrie. 'The playback,' he said. 'Run it for him, Curtis. We don't want to smell his sweat all night.'

A recorder was produced, placed on the desk and set going. Hissing changed to dialling clicks, to the continental ringing tone, to a final harsh click.

'Clichy nine-one, nine-six, seven-six.'

'This is Robert the Bruce,' Petrie's voice said. 'I've a message for Burgundy. You're to tell him that the market was busy and we've transferred the shares.'

'Understood Robert the Bruce. Here is market news for Stockbroker. Dollar shares are strong but Bastille stock still to be negotiated.'

'Understood Burgundy.'

Curtis rushed tape, restarted the playback. This time there were no preliminaries, just the click of a picked up phone.

'Kelvin three-treble-six-three,' Petrie's voice said.

'Stockbroker here,' a plangent voice replied. 'Have you news from Burgundy?'

'Aye, there's a message. Dollar shares are strong but the other stock's sticking.'

'Ach, tell them to get on with it!' the plangent voice said. 'Tell them I say we're on a kittle market. And Robbie.'

'Aye?'

'Watch your back, my man. The longer it goes, the tighter it gets.'

Curtis switched off. Empton inhaled.

'Any comment?' he said to nowhere.

'It wasn't my voice there!' Petrie whined.

'Oh dear,' Empton said. 'Oh dear.'

'But I'm telling you it wasn't.'

'Yes,' Empton said. 'We had a camera on your office window, old chap. You're only hearing the sound effects. What excellent advice that was from McGash.'

'I don't know any McGash!'

'McGash,' Empton said. 'Who'll love to hear you sold him down the river. You'd better start begging for a charge Petrie. I can promise you twenty safe years in Barlinnie.'

Petrie's eyes were starting. 'But what have I done! It isn't a crime to talk to a broker.'

'Ha, ha,' Empton said. No doubt you have several. Between ringing cars and collecting pay-offs.'

He lit a second cigarette from his first. He leaned forward till his face was a foot from Petrie's. He sucked long and thoughtfully then drove smoke full into Petrie's eyes.

'Now,' he said. 'We'll talk, Petrie.'

Petrie dashed at his streaming eyes. 'I've nothing to say.'

'Oh yes,' Empton said. 'I think you'll be saying quite a lot. For one thing I'm a man of my word, and if McGash gets clear you'll be on his list. You'll be a scared man, Petrie, and then a dead man, Petrie, and may be not dead as soon as you could wish. One night a door will open and there he'll be standing and that will be the start of an interesting evening. So that's why you'll be talking, old chap, even if you talk yourself into Barlinnie.' He drew smoke and blew it over Petrie's head. 'On the other hand,' he said. 'I'm a reasonable bastard. A bit of a knockabout man perhaps, but nothing you can't limp away from. Do me a favour and I'll do you one. A couple of words may be enough. I'm not a vindictive man, Petrie – just a bastard who gets what he wants.' He nostrilled smoke. 'So what about it?'

Petrie sat with muzzy eyes, yellow teeth showing between gapped lips. His coarse face was wet with sweat and sweat shone on his freckled hands.

Stupidly he shook his head.

'How I waste my breath,' Empton said. 'But one more attempt at sweet reason before I return you to Curtis and Meaker. You like their company don't you, Petrie?'

Petrie shuddered; he hugged the chair.

'Yes,' Empton said. 'So once again – what about it?'

'I can't – I can't.'

'Easily,' Empton said. 'In so many words – where is McGash?'

'I don't know where.'

'Better,' Empton said. 'Then let's have a very accurate guess.'

'I don't know – I daren't!'

'Oh, I think you dare. He'll never come back to ask who told us.'

Petrie shrank into the chair, mouth quivering. But at last he clamped it tight and shook his head.

Empton scrubbed his cigarette on the desk.

'Right,' he said. 'What a pity, Petrie. You seem to have trouble in understanding me, but doubtless a breath of night air will clear your head.' He nodded to Curtis and Meaker. 'Take him for a drive.'

'No!' Petrie gasped. 'You can't do that.'

'Take him,' Empton said.

'Those bastards will kill me!'

'Not they,' Empton said. 'I trained them myself.'

'I won't go—you can't—!'

The two men grabbed him. He held on to the chair. One of the men jerked it from him. He threw himself down, was snatched up again and his arms twisted hard behind him. Guthrie jumped up.

'That's enough!'

'Don't interfere old man,' Empton said.

'I'm in charge here,' Guthrie said. 'If that man is in custody he's in my custody.'

'Oh no,' Empton said. 'My authority pre-empts you. Sit down old man, or you'll be in trouble.'

'It doesn't', Gently said, 'pre-empt me, nor the rules for the proper treatment of those in custody.'

'Oh halleluiah,' Empton said. 'If you sing Rule Britannia I'll throw up. That bastard can tell us where McGash is, if he talks we can have that wollie-blaster tonight.'

'What is Petrie charged with?'

'Crap on charges,' Empton said. 'The AT Act doesn't need any charges.'

'Neither does it set aside the constituted authority,' Gently said. 'When Petrie leaves this room he goes to a cell.'

'So a drive, so a cell – with Curtis and Meaker!'

'With', Gently said, 'a duty officer. To this authority he has been brought and responsibility for him is with this authority.' He turned to Guthrie. 'We've done with Petrie. He can be admitted and given a cell. Should he be reinterrogated it will be in the presence of a senior officer.'

'You bet,' Guthrie said. 'You bet.' He rapped an order through the intercom.

'By God I'll break you for this,' Empton said. 'I'll have you recalled. Your feet won't touch.'

Gently hunched. 'You can try,' he said. 'The French have a consul in the town.'

'Never mind the French, old man. Any more dead wollies are down to you.'

'And Barentin's safety to both of us,' Gently said.

'Ha, ha,' Empton said. 'Watch your back too.'

A sergeant and a constable came. Petrie was marched off to be booked in. Empton stood glaring. Finally he snarled:

'So we're guessing again. Fetch in maps!'

The girl in the canteen poured their coffee, yawned, went back to her paperback. A couple of patrolmen with plates of egg and chips were the only other occupants of the place. The atmosphere was warm, smelled of coffee, frying; an Espresso machine murmured behind the counter. Guthrie carried the cups. They sat down by a wall poster exhibiting a topless nude.

'Holy Andrew,' Guthrie said. 'But we both stuck our necks out there, man.'

Gently stirred in sugar. 'It isn't the first time we've crossed swords.'

'Can he do what he says?'

Gently drank, shook his head. 'He's got too much sense to try. Empton isn't stupid.'

'For certain he isn't.' Guthrie's eyes were rounded. 'And that's what frightens me about him, man. He's clever as sin and twice as immoral. He'd have had me shooting McGash at sight.' Guthrie paused. 'Not that I mightn't.'

'You wouldn't,' Gently said.

'I'd be tempted. And that black-hearted heathen knew it. He was all for egging me on and giving me reasons why I should.'

Gently drank. 'We must get McGash first.'

'Aye,' Guthrie said. 'So I've been thinking. But how, man?'

After a while Gently said: 'It may be I'll have another tip.'

'Another tip!'

Gently drank. Mechanically Guthrie drank too. The two patrolmen took their plates to the counter and, with a quip to the girl, left. The Espresso machine gurgled: the girl came languidly to fetch the plates.

'Hénault wants out,' Gently said.

'The devil,' Guthrie said. 'Then the chiel came close to it.'

'Close enough. Hénault didn't know the score, thought he'd been chartered for a smuggling run. Now he's playing along but convinced that he's for it at the end of the ride.'

Guthrie whistled softly. 'Sooner him than me! But am I to be told how he's making contact?'

Gently considered his cup for some moments, drank, said: 'Through his former wife.'

'My stars. He was closer still.'

'Hénault got to a phone at Invergarry. He rang her, asked for help, told her to wait at Invergarry Hotel. There was another call, indicating the cottage. She passed it to Frénaye, who passed it to me. That was late last night, after the shooting. Today we went to find the cottage.'

Guthrie gazed at him. 'That former wife sounds a bit of a lassie.'

'I'm not supposed to know she's here,' Gently said. 'Her contact's Frénaye. She won't see me.'

'But does she know what she's playing with?'

'She does now,' Gently said. 'Frénaye warned her off anything reckless. But there's a complication. Barentin has been kind to her. She might take risks for him that she wouldn't for Hénault.'

Guthrie kept gazing. 'You know her well, this lass?'

Gently's shoulder moved. 'It's a long story. She was implicated quite innocently in the Starnberg affair, so getting to know Frénaye, Barentin, myself.'

'And you would not see harm come to her?'

Gently said: 'No.'

Guthrie dropped his eyes to his cup. 'Perhaps I should talk to her.'

'Then we'll lose our contact. After the last time she doesn't trust counter-Intelligence agents.'

'Ach,' Guthrie said. 'Then that makes two of us.' He drained his cup, glanced to the counter. The girl was washing plates, a cigarette stuck to her lip. Guthrie leaned closer. 'So what's it to be?'

'We wait for a fresh call,' Gently said. 'It may or may not come. But Hénault will be desperate after the shooting.'

'And when it comes?'

'Discreet reconnaissance.'

'Aye,' Guthrie nodded.

'That will be my job. When we've cased the set-up we can see if a rescue bid is possible.'

'It'll be a tricksy business,' Guthrie said.

'We had our warning at the cottage,' Gently said. 'Perhaps nothing will be possible, and Empton's right so far – I don't want other Dickies on my conscience. What we have to plan is a way to draw them off, to trick them into leaving Barentin with Hénault. But they may not trust Hénault that far. Unless we're clever they may shoot him first.'

Guthrie kneaded his cup. 'Do you have such a plan?'

Gently said: 'It may involve an open approach.'

Guthrie hissed through his teeth. 'You, man?'

'It would be a job for a senior officer.'

Gently drank up; the Espresso machine simmered; Guthrie kept trying to balance the cup. Some men came in laughing, indulging in horseplay. Then they saw Guthrie and shut up.

Guthrie said: 'It's me for that job.'

Gently shook his head. 'Me. I was instrumental in the Starnberg affair. Talking to me may throw McGash off his guard.'

'But you he'll never spare.'

'I shall hope to be covered.'

'Man, you'll be dead before you can blink.'

'If McGash feels secure he'll want to talk first. If only to gloat at having me at his mercy.'

Guthrie slammed down the cup. 'No, man! I cannot permit such wildish schemes. Dickie was enough, we'll think of other ways. I will not see a man like yourself gunned down.'

Gently shrugged. 'The alternative is Empton's.'

'Aye – and perhaps it's best after all!'

'Barentin's death could trigger many more.'

'Even so,' Guthrie said. 'Even so.'

Gently stared at his cup. The men had got their plates. They were eating in silence at a table across the room. They kept their eyes averted from Gently and Guthrie. Humming to herself, the girl was wiping down the counter.

'But there'll still be liaison?' Guthrie said.

Gently said: 'I must stay in charge.'

'Aye,' Guthrie said. 'But I'll be informed?'

After a pause, Gently nodded.

'My God what a business,' Guthrie said. 'And dumped down from nowhere on my doorstep. Why the hell did those bastards pick my manor?'

'It's one world,' Gently said. 'Old man.'

The desk in hotel reception was deserted and the public rooms were dark, but one caught the aroma of Frénaye's tobacco; he rose from a settee as Gently came in.

'Monsieur has had no trouble ...?'

Gently grunted. 'Have you seen Empton?'

'He came in half an hour since, monsieur. He asked me a number of questions, but I had difficulty in understanding his French.'

'Huh,' Gently said. He plumped down on the settee and lit his own pipe, which tasted foul. Frénaye remained hovering. Reception was shadowy, lit by one bulb.

'Well?'

'No message monsieur. In the morning I will try again.'

'Did you pass on the news?'

'I thought it best, though I regret to say that it caused great concern.'

Gently puffed fiercely. 'Look Frénaye! I saw that car this afternoon.'

'A car, monsieur ...?'

'Her car. She was up the glen and you know it.'

Frénaye also sat; he kept his face to the shadows.

'Monsieur, the call I made was of some length. I spoke with great feeling of a certain matter, and pointed out the difficulty of further concealment. Thus I was empowered, if pressed, to acknowledge my informant's identity, but, at the same time, to make you understand that you must refrain from seeking a meeting. Monsieur, this fills me with great sadness. But I could exact no other concession.'

'You spoke to her this afternoon?'

'Briefly monsieur. She was in fear of a confrontation.'

'What was she doing there?'

'She had grown impatient at receiving no further message from Hénault. She did not know where he was, but guessed it was somewhere in Glengarrry.'

Gently drew bitter smoke. 'How did she seem?'

'Very nervous, monsieur,' Frénaye said. 'One must not forget that she spends her time alone in the hotel, waiting for a call.'

'Did she mention me?'

'To ask where you were.'

'And – this evening?'

Frénaye sank his head. 'I spoke of your great attachment, monsieur. She did not interrupt, but made no reply.'

'Suppose I ... rang her?'

Frénaye gestured a negative. 'Monsieur, my counsel must still be patience. The wound will heal, but as yet it has not. Monsieur's regard is best shown by forbearance.'

Later he stood by his window again, looking out at the river and sleeping town. Rain made the streetlights tender; it fell from a sky like black velvet.

6

It was still raining on Friday morning when Gently crossed the bridge into town. A dreary wrack, like greasy smoke, was puffing across the sky and out to sea. Tourists, shoppers, wore 'impermeables' and hovered in doorways to raise umbrellas; from traffic queued at the lights came the steady thud of wipers. Buildings looked sullen and grimy; the slate roofs had a glint like slime.

In his office Guthrie sat alone. 'The Great Man has cleared off to Fort Augustus,' he said.

'To Fort Augustus ...?'

'He was in here earlier having another go at Petrie.' Guthrie made a face. 'You can't help admiring him, he's a right clever bastard. This morning he was a different man. He was talking to Petrie like a brother.'

'Did it pay off?'

'Enough. Petrie wasn't putting his finger on the map. But Empton trapped him into a couple of admissions, that McGash was out west and that he hadn't gone far.'

Gently hunched.

'You think Petrie was codding him?'

'I think Petrie's more scared of McGash than of Empton.'

'I wonder,' Guthrie said. 'But I was sitting in, and I must say Petrie convinced me. Still, it's nice to think of the Great Man being strung along, it warms one to Petrie. I'll send him in some fags.' Guthrie grinned. 'But what about yourself man?'

'Nothing yet,' Gently said.

'Have you spoken to the lady?'

'Frénaye spoke to her. The last message was two days ago.'

'Two days.' Guthrie blew out his cheeks. 'That's worrisome, man, worrisome. Hénault was playing a queer game, and he's dead for sure if they've rumbled him.'

'It may be he can't get his hands on a phone.'

'Maybe,' Guthrie said, with small conviction. 'But what will you do man, if you've lost your contact?'

Gently humped his shoulders and stared at the rain.

'What area is Empton searching?'

'Ach,' Guthrie said, 'you ken Empton. He's going through every glen from Morvern to Shiel, and double checking around Glengarry.'

'Including Invergarry.'

Guthrie's grey eyes were shrewd. 'You're bothered he might happen on the lady?'

'I'm bothered.'

'Aye,' Guthrie said. 'Then in that case perhaps you should warn her.'

Gently stared a little longer at the rain.

'If I may I'll use your phone.'

. He rang Frénaye but there was nothing fresh. Gently went to collect his car.

He drove without any plan, merely an urgency to be somewhere on the spot. After a sleepless night he'd realized that Frénaye was right and that it might be disastrous to force a meeting. He was still that man who must forgive her but whose forgiveness she couldn't accept: because she couldn't yet forgive herself. Only when that happened would the shadow pass away.

So he must wait, the first move must be hers. He couldn't tell her than none of it mattered: that where they stood contrition, forgiveness were so many words without meaning. Only they themselves had meaning, he, she, caught in an endless moment. But he couldn't tell her: she must find her way back to it; to speak it there were no words.

He drove, scarcely noticing, by the rain-washed pallor of Ness, the wheel continually kicking as swashes of water rose from his tyres. The hills opposite were black, the sky ahead solid darkness: rain bowed the pink spires of foxglove and battered the waving stands of ragwort. Today few cars hugged the shelterless laybys or disputed rights at passing places. Today no hikers filed along the road, though rain-lashed tents stood deserted in a meadow. In a way, the weather suited his mood: to be driving in dark and rain towards ...

Fort Augustus appeared below. In minutes he was down there,

passing the police station. A couple of patrol cars stood before it into one of which a crew was just scrambling. Was it possible that Empton was on to him? He watched in his mirror; the car was following. It came up close. Still in the mirror, he could see the crew discussing together. At the delimit sign he speeded up only slightly and still the patrol car ambled behind him; but then, as they entered a straight, it flashed and swept by. A coincidence? He trod on the gas, kept the patrol car in his sights. It was boring along at sixty in the heart of a mist of spray. All the way to Invergarry he pursued it, saw it cross the bridge and proceed southwards; then, hand on flasher, he checked his mirror – to find a second patrol car behind him! Cursing, he drove on past the ruined castle and out into country. At the first straight he slowed, when the second car at once overtook ...

He let it disappear in the distance before looking for a gap in which to turn. But this was ridiculous! He was behaving like a wanted man on the run. At the same time he was starkly aware of being there without a destination or settled purpose. For if Empton's enquiries reached the hotel, what practical intervention could he make?

He drove back slowly into the village, alert for further signs of police presence. Having made his turn he kept straight on, past the hotel, past the shop. Nothing: nobody: rain had swept the place clean. He turned once more, using the verge. Now the hotel was directly in front of him, pale walls, dark roof, lights showing in some windows. Was there a watcher? He held his face averted as the building drew closer, then swung off into the layby and the shadow of the trees. The layby was probably part of an old road: it was almost, not quite, opposite the hotel. He drifted in under the trees as far as he could get and switched off wipers and engine.

So he was there: as near as he dared go!

But now the situation seemed even more preposterous. A few rainy yards across grass, road, gravel and he could be with her, sweeping her into his arms. So why wait? The absurdity galled him. He reached out for the door-handle. Impossible that, if they met face to face ... her eyes imprisoned by his own ... But then, as though a switch flicked, he was seeing that other image of Gabrielle, the eyes staring with horror and loathing, the violence of hands, of voice ... He shuddered and let go the handle: there could be no short cut to obliterating that! It had happened and had nearly destroyed her; it must be lived out, left to wither in its course ...

Doggedly he lit his pipe and set himself to wait and watch. On balance it was probably unlikely that Empton would waste much time on Glengarry. The glen had been the focus of attention yesterday after the discovery of the body, patrols had been up to Kinloch Hourn, there was doubtless still a presence at the cottage. But the affair was no mystery and called for no investigation in depth; while the least likely place for a second safe house would be up the glen or in the village. Empton, no fool, might put in a patrol as cover against the unexpected, but himself and his major resources would be directed elsewhere. That was the logic of it; so why did he, Gently, feel an unease about the situation – a need to stake out here, as though a crisis threatened that he could only sense in his bones? Because sense it he did: he had no other reason to sit there in the rain. He had been, he had checked, the coast was clear, and to remain there so close to her now was a torment ...

Meanwhile the hotel continued isolated in rain. No one came, no one left. He could see the roofs of cars above the wall that screened the yard, but not so well that he could pick out the little Citroën. Now and then he caught a movement behind a rain-smeared window; at one he could dimly see a chef at his work. Cars passed, one trailing a big caravan, but none stopped or even slowed. It was approaching the lunch hour and he, like a fool, hadn't brought as much as a packet of crisps. He knocked out his pipe, refilled it; knocked it out, refilled it again ...

Then a car did stop and, at once alert, he recognized the two men in it as reporters; no doubt they had been to the cottage to drum up copy, take photographs. The driver glanced towards him: he turned his head. The car continued into the hotel yard. A lunch stop of course – yet, being reporters, could they refrain from firing a few questions? he scowled over his pipe. If they had recognized him they might put two and two together: then, appraising the other diners, begin to take notice of the solitary French girl ... In effect his being there was a liability and might catch the attention not only of reporters. He chewed hard at his pipe. But he would stay! His intuition had hardened into obstinacy.

Another car appeared, pulled into the layby and parked provokingly just behind him. In his mirror he saw a middle-aged lady wearing a head scarf get out and run to fetch a basket from the boot. He sank even deeper into his seat. He watched them unwrap sandwiches, pour tea from a thermos. They sent curious looks at the car ahead of them and the slumped figure of its driver, chatted, laughed. So what did they take him for, brooding there in the rain? Probably anything but a policeman! The man, a short pudgy-featured fellow, looked like a tax man or a solicitor's clerk.

Irrationally irritated, Gently got out and made an act of stretching; then, keeping his back to the hotel, strolled a few steps under the dripping trees. Fifty feet below purled the Garry river, in spate from so much rain; behind him, he judged, if he turned, he might just get a glimpse of the cars in the yard. He turned. His heart thumped! He was staring at Gabrielle! Also wearing a head scarf, she was stooping to unlock her car. Hardly knowing what he did, he jumped, stumbled down the bank under the trees, froze listening, heard the car door plunk, the starter skirl, the Citroën's twin begin chattering. Closer it sounded, paused, accelerated and departed towards the junction; starting up through the trees he was in time to see the car flashing the turn to Fort Augustus. He raced to the Marina. The picnic couple were staring at him wide-eyed. He jumped into his car, spun the engine and shot away with squealing tyres.

It had been too sudden.

His movements mechanical, he drove for some distance in complete stupor. His brain was refusing to catch up, was still back in the layby, dulled with waiting. Yet he must have seen her: it must have happened: he must now be chasing her towards Fort Augustus ... in the flesh, Gabrielle! No longer a memory, but a woman stooping to unlock her car.

Almost it had been too real, that vision of the slightly-stocky figure; of the softly-stern profile, the proud set of head and shoulders. French: it belonged to France; how could it appear here so inconsequentially? He felt a lightness, a weakness; a sense of the present being a dream.

But a sight of her car brought him back to himself: he'd surely been driving like a madman! He eased his pedal to give the bobbing Citroën a good two hundred yards grace. Nevertheless he could see her scarfed head, could imagine her hands on the wide, ribbed wheel, her neat foot pressing the organ-pedal ... as, once before, in time lost ... He drove the image from his mind. Now, somehow, he must take a grip on the present ...

For where was she going?

Brow creased in a frown, he set himself to marshal the possibilities. An innocent visit to Fort Augustus was by far the most likely. She couldn't stay for ever minding the phone, and Fort Augustus was the nearest town; if she had needs that the village store couldn't supply, then Fort Augustus provided the answer. But if not Fort Augustus? Beyond that town all roads led to Inverness; at Inverness there was Frénaye: at Inverness there might also be himself!

He felt his cheeks flush at the thought, but immediately he dismissed it. If her destination was Inverness she would be going to see Frénaye, with whom she had doubtless made a rendezvous. Yet why? Why wouldn't the phone do? And why risk leaving her post for so long? Had she received a message that involved her so deeply that simply to relay it wasn't enough?

He checked his speed again: he'd let it race with his thoughts till the gap between the cars had almost halved. Now they were running into the town and she was slowing at the limit signs. The police station passed, its forecourt empty; ahead, the road turned left into town; there also was the junction of the Dores road, obscure, apparently leading only to the abbey and the school. The Citroën slowed almost to a stop and he could see her head turn, seeking a sign; then the car moved forward tentatively, flashed, and wheeled into the Dores road. Not a shopping trip! But then where? The main road to Inverness ran through the town. Unless she had been studying a map, could she guess that the minor road also led there?

He flashed and followed. The Citroën was crawling, still confused by the beckoning abbey. But at last it latched on to the A862 and began to pick up speed again. Houses faded, they passed the top end of Ness, commenced the long haul away from the strath; and still the Citroën chugged on sturdily, an intent little car quite certain where it was going. Not to Fort Augustus, not to Inverness: and from this road stretched the tangle of the back country: the minor hill roads that connected scattered settlements between Loch Ness and the untamed Monadhliaths. Was that her objective? Or the distant A9 ... a few miles from where the whole affair had started?

Here the country was open, the traffic slight, and he was obliged to stay at long distance. It fretted him that whenever she was out of sight she might be disappearing down some side-track. She wasn't in a hurry. After the grind from the strath she'd settled down to between thirty and forty, the small car bouncing amiably over the rugged surfaces and heeling visibly on the bends. Was she conscious of being followed? He was glad when occasional cars overtook them; but overtaking wasn't easy, and when he let a car by it often stuck behind her for over a mile. Once she must have slowed, since he turned a bend to find himself almost brushing the Citroën's tall stern: he braked at once, ducking his head. But she gave no sign that she'd noticed him.

They passed the junction to Foyers: still she clung to the A862. In distant convoy they skirted Loch Mohr, grey with rain, its hills untidy. Then Errogie; then a critical junction with a road that led to the A9; then Torness, and a smaller loch overlooked by grey crags. Was it to be Inverness after all? In a few miles more they'd be dropping down to Dores. Already they'd driven most of the length of Ness, hidden behind the streaming hills. Yet on she puttered, slow, certain, the scarfed head facing always before. Always the Citroën disappeared round a bend to reappear, steaming steadily ahead.

And then, quite suddenly, it didn't! The road stretched ahead with no car visible! In an instant he jammed on brakes, jumped out, began hastily staring about him. He'd just turned a bend: the road was dropping down to another big loch with a farmhouse close to it. But the farmhouse she couldn't have reached, and the road for half a mile beyond was quite empty. It was baffling. For a moment it seemed that the landscape had swallowed her up.

Then his eye caught a movement deep down on his right, where trees clothed the foot of a craggy hill. He stared incredulously – yes, it was the Citroën, still bobbing along where no road seemed to be. But a road there was. What appeared to be a farm track slanted recklessly down from a point above him: it was unsigned, and he had missed it in his surprise at losing sight of the Citroën.

He dived back into the car, reversed hard and wound round into the unpromising track. It plunged down past sheep hurdling, through mud and dung, humped over a stone bridge, then entered the trees. Not a farm track: though narrow and tortuous, it had a regular tarmac surface. What he desperately needed was a glimpse of the map, but he dared not delay for such enlightenment. By now she must be half a mile ahead, and possibly arriving at her destination ...

He drove furiously, but the tiny road seemed designed to check all haste. It wound up, down and around, with wrong-way cambers and deformed surfaces. He cleared the trees. Across moorland ahead rose the folding, rounded heights of the Monadhliaths, with before them yet one more loch, its far shore steep and crag-fast. Then left, and quite close, a set of flattish hairpins, up which the Citroën was making its inexorable way: apparently the approach to an isolated farmhouse that stood against the sky, beside it a tree. Here ...? He eased off again. But the road, the Citroën carried on past the farmhouse. Reaching it, one saw the road ribboning away, for a while straight, in line with the loch shore.

And still no hurry! But the map she must have studied to have picked up that junction at the first time of asking. Without doubt her destination was pinpointed; and what source could have pinpointed it for her, but one? Had she rung Frénaye? Did she mean to ring him ...? Gently felt himself growing more and more uneasy. Careless now whether she spotted him or not, he drew up to within fifty yards of the Citroën.

The loch ended; the road bore right. At the bend stood a house at a higher level. Of modern construction, it was most likely a fishing lodge for anglers visiting the loch; a short, steep drive led to it from a hardstanding at the roadside. The house came towards them. The Citroën didn't falter, but Gently saw the scarfed head turn. In a flash he had turned too, was taking a mental photograph of the white-painted house. Blank windows, closed door, a veranda on which no fishing rods stood: but also the chocolate-brown muzzle of a Volvo poking round the side of the house. No people: no movement; he stared at the place again in his mirror. It loomed high, niched into moorland: it had ranging visibility in every direction. Gabrielle drove on. He drove on. In the distance two houses: one appeared to be a shop.

The shop and house stood on an elevated apron around which the road made an eccentric loop; between them lay a parking area, and on this Gabrielle turned the Citroën. Face averted, Gently continued till the house hid his car from view; then he pulled into the verge, grabbed glasses, got out and scrambled up the bank by the house. He could see the parking area through shrubs. Gabrielle was standing by her car. She also had glasses; the glasses were trained on the fishing lodge back down the road. Absorbed, ignoring the mizzle, she gazed at the distant house, then lowered the glasses and gazed again; raised them, and continued her survey. A figure at once independent and vulnerable ... he yearned to hasten to her, catch her in his arms! It seemed intolerable to cling there watching her, somehow shameful: an act of betrayal.

But at last she was satisfied and put away the glasses. By the corner of the shop was a phone box; she went into the box, took coins from a purse, began dialling a number she didn't have to look up. The call was short; she returned to the Citroën. She drove through the parking and rejoined the road. Crouching by his fence, Gently could see the little car drive up to a T-junction, flash and turn right. He didn't attempt to follow. He guessed now where he was; the road she had taken was heading back to Fort Augustus. She had been, she had seen, and wasn't making the mistake of passing by that house again ...

He dropped off the bank and walked round to the parking, where the shop turned out to sell only craft goods. A long, low building converted from a cow shed, it also rented boats and fishing gear. He went in. A woman appeared from among the stalls of woollens and jewellery. Nodding in the direction of the fishing lodge, Gently said:

'Any chance of renting that property by the loch?'

'Well now,' the woman said. 'You should have walked in here last week. You might have had it for a fortnight then, but now it's rented through to October.' She smiled apologetically; her accent had been a surprise.

'Someone else took it?'

'Too right,' she said. 'You get a chance booking once in a while. A fella dropped in here last Friday and asked if it was vacant, name of Robertson.'

'Robertson,' Gently said. 'I used to know a Robertson. A short, plump man with a Glasgow accent.'

'Naow,' the woman said. 'This wouldn't be him. You wouldn't call him short, just kind of ordinary. He paid cash and left a Liverpool address, and what would I know about his accent?' She grinned. 'We're from down under,' she said. 'My man took a job here managing sheep.'

'Is Robertson in occupation now?' Gently said.

'Yeah,' she said. 'It's let Wednesday to Wednesday. They rang us Wednesday evening, said they'd be late and would I leave it unlocked. That's no sweat, the folk around here are honest. Reckon you'll find him there if you want him.'

'Wednesday,' Gently said. 'He hasn't dropped by since.'

'Not with it raining wombats,' the woman said wryly. 'I haven't let a boat these two days. But they'll be around when it stops.'

'Is there a store handy if I rented the property?'

'Down the road and turn right. You'll come to the post office.'

The property was called Camghouran, she told him, and the name of the loch was Loch Ruthven. Gently thanked her and bought a nugget of rough amethyst from a tray on the counter. He went outside. With his back planted against the phone box he made a survey of the lodge with glasses. The site had been let into rising ground which to the rear reached the level of the first floor windows. Here there was birch scrub. The moor round about had bush heather, bilberry. Down by the road was more birch scrub, perhaps enough to screen a car left on the hard-standing. Cover: but not much cover. On the moor he noted a couple of boulders. For a mile one way, half a mile the other, the road came under surveillance from the big windows.

He returned to the car, drove to the junction, turned right and found the post office. A smaller establishment than that at Invergarry, it was nevertheless equipped with a phone booth. A man, a woman, were unpacking cartons: Gently produced the photocopy of Hénault.

'Police. Has this man been in here lately? He may not now have a moustache.'

They looked at it, glanced at each other.

'Is he a Frenchman?' the woman said.

'When did he come in?'

'This morning,' the man said. 'About midday. If it's him.'

'Alone?'

'He came in alone, but there was another man waiting in a car.'

'Did you get a look at the other man?'

'Ach, no! I was busy just then with pensions. But I saw the car, a brown Volvo – it pulled up a wee bit further on.'

'I served the Frenchman,' the woman said. 'He brought in a list of groceries a mile long – ach, enough for a family for a week, and whisky too. It came to a bit.'

'Did he use the phone?'

'Aye – I had to give him change for a five-pound note. But what's he done?'

Gently put away the picture. 'Just routine enquiries,' he said.

He went to the phone booth, rang the hotel. Frénaye was quickly on the line.

'Listen Frénaye. Has there been a call within the last half hour?'

'But monsieur! How could you know—?'

'Was there?'

'It was half an hour ago precisely, monsieur.'

'And?'

'I regret no message. The lady I thought sounded despondent.'

'No message.'

'It was my impression that the lady has given up hope. But, monsieur—'

'Thanks,' Gently said. 'See you soon.' He hung up.

Back in the car he pored over a map, then sat for a while listening to the rain. The sky overhead was solid murk and cars passed rarely on the narrow road. At last he lit his pipe, fired the engine, turned and drove away north. He passed the junction. Soon the shop, the white house were left behind in the gloom and the rain.

7

He took the B861 back to Inverness, a road that opened great
prospects of the town and its hills. By the time he reached it the
rain had slackened, though still the wrack was dark and low. At
the bridge he hesitated, drove on and turned, traversed the one-
way and parked at the police station. He went in and knocked at
Guthrie's office: found it occupied only by Empton and his man
Curtis.

'Where's Guthrie?' Gently asked.

Empton was laying down the phone. His vulturine features had
a flush and his eyes were mean with anger.

'So what's it to you old man?' he snapped. 'Or are you helping
out now with the amateur connection?'

'What amateur connection?'

'Ask around. But he's taken bloody manpower I need here.'

'What amateur connection?' Gently asked Curtis.

'A job at Aviemore, sir,' Curtis said bleakly. 'A bird got herself
raped and strangled. The Chief Super's gone out there.'

'And that's what you call an amateur job?'

'Ha, ha,' Empton said. 'Don't make me spit.' He got up from
Guthrie's chair and came to stare into Gently's face. 'Old man,' he
said, 'I could kill you, and that's not a figure of speech. I've just
had the top man trampling on my goolies for pussyfooting
around with Petrie. The Frogs have been at him. They're
screaming for blood because I've cut McGash's line with Paris.
The Frogs are soft, they want to deal, but the wogs won't play till
they reestablish contact. My head's on the block, and whose to
blame? Old man pick your moment, but drop dead.'

Gently stared back at him. 'You knew the risk.'

'Risk, risk,' Empton said. 'I could have had it out of Petrie last
night and never left a mark on him. That's why they pay me, what
I do. We could have been back in London old man. Instead we're
just a wollie short and me up the creek without a paddle.' His teeth

showed in a snarl. 'And the Frogs still love you,' he said. 'Don't think I didn't try to drop you in it. One day you won't be made of asbestos.'

'So when is Guthrie due back,' Gently said.

'To hell with Guthrie,' Empton said. 'I want that Frog of yours. I want him here. If he knows something he's going to spill it.'

'He knows nothing further.'

'Lovely boy,' Empton said. 'And if he did would you tell me? But he'll spill what he does know. He had a tip from somewhere, and that somewhere I want my hands on.'

'He is entitled to protect his source.'

'Listen,' Empton said, 'before I throw up. There's only one source he could get a grass from, and that's your fancy bit in Rouen. Who was in Rouen. Who isn't in Rouen. Because I made it my business to check. So guess where she is now, at this very moment, and what she's doing, and who she's reporting to. Go on, have a guess on me – then get that Frog round here double quick.'

'He brought information,' Gently said. 'He has no further information.'

'But you know where she is,' Empton said. 'You know, because you wouldn't not know, you wouldn't let the Frog hold out on that. So where is she?'

'Frénaye's source is protected.'

'And you think I'll go on chasing my arse?'

'Any additional information will be acted upon.'

Empton looked as though he would hit him.

'Get Petrie in here!'

'Wait,' Gently said. He went to the intercom, asked for Tate. Tate came in. 'The Superintendent wishes to reinterrogate Petrie,' Gently said.

'All right!' Empton snarled. 'Play your game. But don't forget I'm going to play mine too. Watch out for your Frog, watch out for your girl friend, because I'll have them if they put a foot wrong. And meanwhile, old man, I do have Petrie, whether we go by the book or not. And I'm going to break him if it takes all night and a whole deck of senior officers.'

'That's your privilege,' Gently said.

'Yeah, that's my privilege,' Empton said.

Petrie was fetched. With him came a CID officer who identified himself as a Chief Inspector Muirhead. He signalled one of Petrie's escort to remain and himself took a seat by the desk. Gently left with Tate. When they were clear of the office he took the Inspector by the arm:

'On my own authority, no questions asked, I want another gun and some CS grenades.'

Tate stared at him with eyes gone still.

'I don't know if I can, sir ... just like that.'

'You can,' Gently said. 'My writ runs as far as that gentleman's back there.'

'But ... what's it about, sir?'

'No questions, no answers. I'll leave a note for you to hand to Guthrie. You say nothing to nobody.'

'Well ... I don't know, sir ...'

'I'll be waiting in the incident room.'

The incident room was still a busy place with reports in the pipe line from distant searchers. Gently found a seat amongst the hubbub and scribbled a few lines for Guthrie. He sealed them in an envelope, addressed it, added 'Strictly FYEO'. He waited. Ten minutes later Tate appeared carrying a canvas grip.

'Would you sign this quittance, sir.'

Gently signed it. Still Tate seemed reluctant to deliver the grip.

'If you could give me a hint, sir ...'

Gently shook his head, held out his hand and took the grip.

'Just one thing. Later on tonight you may get a call from a French officer named Frénaye. Whatever he asks you to do, see you do it at the double.'

'But sir ...'

'Here's the note for Guthrie.'

Gently went, lugging the grip. It felt heavy; examining it in the car, he found Tate had put in a full case of grenades.

He left the grenades locked in his boot but took the gun with him into the hotel. Frénaye was in reception; after putting in an order for tea, Gently collected the Frenchman and took him upstairs. Frénaye sounded prickly:

'Monsieur, I wish to know—!'

Gently hustled him along to his room. Once inside he put his finger to his lips, then began a frisk of the room. Bug one was behind the radiator, fastened to the wall with Scotch tape. Using his nail file as a screwdriver he removed the base plate of the telephone, and there revealed bug two. Gently slid up the window and looked out. A dumper truck laden with rubble was passing. The two bugs sailed through the air and departed countrywards in the truck.

'The tricky bastard.'

Frénaye was staring. 'It is Monsieur Empton who does this?'

'Later we'll check your room too. Also the telephone in reception.'

He went on searching until he was satisfied that the room held no more bugs. The tea came. Gently poured and fell ravenously on toast and jam. Frénaye sipped tea distantly. Gently finished the toast and began on the pastries. Finally, after gulping more tea, he felt under his jacket and hoisted out the gun.

'Here.'

Frénaye gazed at it. 'A gun for me, monsieur …?'

'For you.'

Frénaye took the gun. He examined it; his eyes had softened.

'Monsieur, please allow me to express …'

Gently shrugged. 'You may have to use it. But now we're quits – once you stuck your neck out to get me a gun when I needed it.'

'At the same time, monsieur—'

'I said you may have to use it. And that time may not be far away.'

He related the day's events. Frénaye listened without interruption. As he listened he toyed with the gun, spun the chambers, hefted it. The gun was familiar in his hand: he was a man who lived with a gun. When Gently ended his account, Frénaye rested the gun on his knee.

'Monsieur is convinced that mademoiselle failed to notice him?'

Gently considered. 'You think she may have?'

Frénaye caressed the gun. 'Monsieur tailed her for many miles, and she could not but be aware that you might seek to observe her. So she leads you to this place, then, an act of defiance, rings to tell me she has no message. This I would not put beyond her monsieur. She is a woman with ways of her own.'

'But what could be the object?'

'Monsieur, it is that you and you only shall know that place. You she trusts. Even I am but a Frenchman in a foreign land, without power or authority.'

Gently shook his head. 'I wish I could believe that. But I was looking at a different picture. She went there to case the lodge, and when she did it she wasn't acting a part.'

Frénaye stroked the gun. 'I could ring her monsieur.'

'Then you'd have to tell her how you knew she was lying.'

'Monsieur, we cannot let her proceed.'

'Monsieur, we must prevent it by taking action ourselves.'

Gently poured, drank more tea. 'We may not have much time,' he said. 'Empton is up there working on Petrie and I wouldn't put it past Empton to crack him. Empton is savage. He has just been reprimanded for breaking the terrorists' link with Paris. If he cracks Petrie there'll be no quarter. And Guthrie's away. We're on our own.'

Frénaye went on fondling the gun. 'Monsieur has a plan?' he asked.

'I've a plan.' Gently got up, fetched paper, began to sketch. 'They're trusting Hénault,' he said. 'Just a little. That's how Hénault is getting to a phone. They think it's safe to let him fetch and carry, he may even be doing a trick as lookout.'

'We cannot be sure of that,' Frénaye said.

'But perhaps we dare rely on this,' Gently said. 'That, if there is a commotion out there near the house, they will leave Barentin with Hénault while they investigate.'

Frénaye was silent, then said: 'What commotion?'

'Here's the lay out,' Gently said. 'The house is below the level of the moor, and there's parking by the gate out of sight of the house. Unless the weather changes right about it will be black as pitch tonight. The bend is on a shallow gradient. We come in without lights, cut engine and coast down to the parking.'

'It is possible,' Frénaye said reluctantly.

'You will wait while I approach the house from the rear. I have CS grenades. From up there, at a pinch, I could lob them through the windows. But that will come later. First, I'm going to draw them. Behind the house is parked the car. I'm going to fire one shot at the car, with any luck getting the windscreen.'

'Is there cover?' Frénaye said.

'A little scrub. But I'm above and they're below. If there's any light it will be behind them, and to get at me they must climb a bank.'

'And then?' Frénaye said.

'Wait,' Gently said. 'Wait until you hear further shooting. Either they'll be shooting at me, or I'll be firing shots to let you know they've come out. When you hear the shooting, go. You'll have your gun and three grenades. Get Barentin and Hénault out of there, down to the car, away.'

'But monsieur!'

'Listen,' Gently said. 'Half a mile on there's a shop and phone box. You'll stop, ring Inverness police, then drive straight on into town.'

'But no monsieur – this is unthinkable!'

'Monsieur, it is essential. I have sufficiently alerted Inverness police and they will take immediate action. Meanwhile we must avoid all risk of Monsieur Barentin's being recaptured.'

Frénaye jumped up agitatedly. 'No monsieur. I cannot, I will not agree to such a plan. Let us have men stationed in the area, properly equipped and ready to move in.'

'Not possible,' Gently said. 'It would need Guthrie, and Guthrie's tied up in Aviemore.'

'In that case monsieur, this Hénault can drive, and I will return after making the phone call.'

'Hénault,' Gently said, 'will be under arrest.'

'Then it is I, Maurice Frénaye, who will provide the diversion.'

'No,' Gently said, 'and no. Because I have made a reconnaissance and you have not.'

Frénaye gestured with the gun. 'Monsieur, I am desolate, but this cannot be. You will be left at the mercy of ruthless men, doubly enraged by the loss of their hostage. Monsieur, I hold your life more precious. Monsieur, you do not think of mademoiselle. Monsieur, your plan is excellent, but we cannot proceed without more men.'

'We cannot have more men.'

'Then we will wait.'

'We cannot wait.'

'Then we must make another plan. Monsieur, you have grenades, we will throw them through the windows, we will take our chance, but we will do it together.'

Gently stared at him, then shook his head. 'Our object is to keep Barentin alive. My way will work. Once they lose Barentin they won't want to waste time hunting me.'

'Monsieur, they will not stop to think of that.'

'Monsieur,' Gently said, 'I am above and they below. There is no wind. That site is a trap. I have only to explode my grenades.'

'First, monsieur may be shot.'

'Monsieur intends to present no target.'

'I do not like it,' Frénaye said. 'I am not happy.' He resumed his seat. 'But monsieur is logical.'

Gently poured more tea; they drank. Frénaye invested in a tea cake. Whenever his dark eyes fell on the gun they took on a softness, a complacency.

'Monsieur, it may be that we shall capture these terrorists.'

'Maybe,' Gently said. 'And maybe alive.'

'On that matter,' Frénaye said, 'you have not changed your opinion?'

'For us,' Gently said, 'can there be two standards?'

Before dinner Gently rang Tate, but Guthrie had not returned from Aviemore. The case, which involved a hostel and its associated sports centre, had a ring of complex routine about it. Empton, Tate told him, was still working on Petrie; as yet he'd heard no whisper of a break-through.

'Has Guthrie been on the line?' Gently asked.

'Yes sir. A short time ago.'

'You said something to him?'

'Well ... yes, sir. He said I was to give you every support.'

Gently hesitated, then hunched. 'Stand by for a call at around ten p.m.'

Waiting: the onerous part. At first his mind had been absorbed by the plan, checking it move by move, the white house vivid before his eye. But came the moment when the details were definitive, the programme instinct in his brain; and then his brain turned its back on it and sought for the image of Gabrielle. Had she indeed been aware of his presence? She could have been on the watch, back in Invergarry. Yet would she have ignored him so completely, so casually, conscious of his closeness at every moment?

Several times he eyed the phone: something she must say to him, if he rang! It wasn't possible that she would just slam the phone down, knowing he was there, feeling his nearness. And even to hear her voice, angry, repulsing, was still to hear the voice of Gabrielle: the voice that had told her love: voice in all the world hers. Yet each time he kept his hand from the phone. Until she wanted it ... until she rang him! Only one thing was certain: he would never let her leave Scotland before, face to face, they had spoken together.

'Monsieur, the rain has almost stopped.'

Frénaye had gone out to stretch his legs; his return marked the end of a blank spell when time had done its best to stand still.

'No risk of the sky clearing?'

'None monsieur. I do not admire your Scottish weather.'

'Let's go into dinner,' Gently grunted.

'Monsieur, I do not think they are yet serving.'

A drink at the bar bridged the gap, and while they ate light leaked from the drab evening. Lamps flicked on along the riverside, cars began passing with dipped lights. And she too would be at her table, in the hotel down the Great Glen: matching him, it might be, thought for thought – though more likely revolving some harebrain exploit. Her reconnaissance was made. At Hénault's next call she would brief him on what to expect; possibly she knew, as they did not, an optimum moment for an attempt. When Hénault was watchdog, when the others slept ... perhaps even some jiggery-pokery with drugs? To her, it must seem credible: worth the risk of staying silent.

Ought he to step in, whether or no? But Hénault's next call could not be today. They had stocked up that morning for several days, would not soon be visiting the store again. Not today, not tomorrow; and the next day was Sunday. Unless Hénault had some other trick for getting to a phone, Monday was the earliest she could make her move ...

'Monsieur,' Frénaye said.

Gently looked up: Empton had entered the dining room. He paused, eyes on their table; then came stalking across.

'Well, well, old man,' he said. He pulled up a chair and sat. 'I'm sure you'd like a progress report,' he said. 'And then again, I'm wondering if you need one.'

Gently said nothing.

'A mute witness,' Empton said. 'But this is the way of it old man. I've just been looking through the reports coming in, and one puts you at Invergarry this morning.'

'So,' Gently said.

'Oh quite,' Empton said. 'Delightful scenery and all that. But scarcely the weather for it, old man. And you do have such a keen ear for whispers.' His eyes were tight on Gently's. 'So what's at Invergarry, old man?' he said. 'Apart from the castle, that you know about, and I don't know about, and don't get told about?'

'I heard you were rechecking the area,' Gently said.

'Charming,' Empton said. 'You were giving me a hand.'

'That you had elicited a hint from Petrie.'

'It brought you running,' Empton said. 'Keep on telling me.'

'Not having any information of my own,' Gently said, 'I took a chance on yours.'

'Oh brilliant,' Empton said. 'Homing in at once on Invergarry.'

'Invergarry,' Gently said, 'seemed a good place to start, being close to the spot where the trail went cold. But I may have been wasting my time. Perhaps Petrie's hints are not to be trusted.'

'Never mind Petrie,' Empton said. 'I've got Petrie's welfare in hand.'

'So sorry if I'm disappointing you,' Gently said.

'Yeah,' Empton said. 'I can imagine.' He glared at Frénaye, then back to Gently. 'Well, well,' he said. 'Always the clever answer. If I wasn't so naive I might think you were foxing me. Perhaps it is only the castle at Invergarry.'

'Is Petrie talking yet?' Gently said.

'Don't bother about him old man,' Empton said. 'We're being kind to him. He's having his supper. Which could mean of course that he's been singing for it. I see you're having yours early.'

'It's the way the weather affects me,' Gently said.

'Joke,' Empton said. 'But stay loose, old man. And don't get too busy around the scene.'

He laughed, got up and left them. They saw him collect a flask from the bar. Then, without another glance, he strode through reception and out into the night.

Frénaye eyed Gently with concern.

'My soul, but that man has a strange effect on me! It is as though I am the rabbit and he the stoat. Monsieur, can it be that he divines our intentions?'

'It can,' Gently grunted. 'By now he must know that his bugs have gone spare. We shall have to watch out for sticking-plasters.'

'Monsieur, must we not also warn mademoiselle?'

After a pause Gently nodded. 'She must leave. It means

breaking contact, but after tonight that shouldn't matter.'

'I will phone her now.'

'Not yet. Empton may be anticipating such a reaction.'

They finished dinner. Back in his room, Gently made a further precautionary check: the room was clean. Frénaye rang, but as he listened his expression changed to one of alarm. He hung up quickly.

'Monsieur, she did not return to the hotel.'

'What!'

'They have not seen her since she went out after lunch.'

Gently stared at him blank-faced: he could feel the blood thump in his temples.

'Then come on. Let's get out there.'

'Oh monsieur! That we are not too late.'

But still a delay – they had to search the car. Frénaye took the inside, Gently the out. Two tracer bugs came to light, one tucked in the rear fender, one placed cunningly under a loose corner of the carpet. A van was parked by the Marina: Gently posted the bugs through its grille. Then they piled in and he wheeled the Marina out of the yard.

'Monsieur, she must have made some arrangement this morning ...'

'Keep your eye open for a tail.'

Over the bridge he'd taken a chance, turned right and eliminated the one-way. Horns had serenaded behind him, but he was safe on the Dores road.

'She would have issued Hénault with instructions ...'

Yes, all that was plain enough now. No waiting till Monday! She'd had a plan simmering over, ready to spring it as soon as she heard from him. This afternoon had been no tentative reconnaissance but a final check for essential detail – then she'd drawn off to wait, like himself, till the fall of night.

And the plan?

He shuddered to think of it, could take her no closer to that frightening peril. Let it not be yet, let it not be yet. Let there still be time to intercept it. ...

'Monsieur, I perceive no tail.'

'Keep watching. He may not rely on his bugs.'

He'd rushed through the suburbs, left the streetlights, was

bucking into the pitchy cavern of the night. Not a road for speed! The car bounced and lurched as he forced the speedometer up to seventy. Nothing showed behind in his mirror, ahead lay only the unreaming road. At Dores they peeled off into the hills, and then the going became truly rough: the Marina banged and bottomed and drifted its tail on bad bends. Still he kept it shifting. They'd met no traffic all the way. They stormed down from Ashie Moor, passed the upper Wade road, soon were skirting crags by Loch Duntelchaig.

'A turn left – watch out for it.'

But from this direction it was easier to spot. Once more he was charging through sheep droppings and slamming into the tiny stone bridge. Four wheels off! Here he had to ease up if he was to stay on the road at all. Swearing to himself, he wriggled and squirmed through the switchback bends among the trees. And then ahead – lights. On this narrowest of all roads, with passing places far to seek: another car dashing towards them, its haste apparent in the bouncing headlights. Fuming, Gently raced ahead. Tyres screeched, the two cars halted bumper to bumper. And suddenly, though its headlights were blinding him, he recognized the shape of a Deux-Chevaux.

'Monsieur – it is Hénault. It is Monsieur Barentin!' They'd piled out of the Marina and run to the Citroën. The driver's scared face, white in the headlights, was that of the photostat in Gently's pocket, while lolling beside him, seemingly unconscious, was the slight figure of the French industrialist.

Gently's hands were on Hénault's collar.

'Where is she – where is Mademoiselle Orbec?'

'Monsieur, I do not know—'

'We are police!' Frénaye snapped. 'You had better tell us quickly what has happened.'

'Monsieur, we are in danger—'

'Talk!' Gently snarled. 'Where is mademoiselle?'

'Monsieur I do not know! She is back at the house – and now – at any moment—'

'You left her there?'

'Monsieur I could not help it. I had to get Monsieur Barentin away. He is helpless, he is drugged, I had to carry him in my arms—'

'She is in their hands?'

'I cannot say. They were hunting for her behind the house. She was screaming, throwing stones at the windows – first one and then the other went after her—'

Gently hauled him from the car. 'Get in the back!'

'But monsieur, they are sure to follow—'

'You're under arrest – get in the back. You are the prisoner of Inspector Frénaye.' To Frénaye he said: 'Take the Citroën, drive to the farmhouse we passed near the junction, alert Inverness, then drive on to town.'

'Oh monsieur—!'

'Do as I say!'

Gently jumped back into the Marina. He reversed savagely, sent it bounding forward over rock and bracken to clear the Citroën. He didn't look back. Ahead were the hairpins, the level going by the loch. The Marina blundered, squealed and slammed at a speed he didn't check. He reached the bend, didn't cut his lights, went straight on in through the gates of the house. The house was unlit. The car had gone. He skidded to a halt, came out with his gun.

'Gabrielle!'

Again, an open door. He rushed it, crouched, kicked it wide. He went in. Nothing: no sound. He swept on lights: empty rooms.

'Gabrielle!'

He raced up the stairs. Nothing stirred in all the house. Below, his car lights lit the granite chippings where the Volvo had stood, but stood no longer.

8

'Ah monsieur, you are safe!'

And after all it was Frénaye who first arrived at the empty house. In obedience to instructions, he had driven to the farmhouse and made his call to Inverness; to be advised then by the farmer that a strapping son of his was himself a special constable. Authority enough: Frénaye had off-loaded his prisoner and charge to the son. Now he'd dumped the Deux-Chevaux below and come running up the drive, gun in hand.

'They have gone, monsieur?'

'Gone.'

'You have searched …?'

'Only the house.'

Though Gently was standing stock still by his car his breath was coming fast. In fact he'd been up on the moor, scrambling about there like one demented, feeling through heather, bracken, birch scrub and praying, praying …

At first his one thought had been pursuit and he'd actually leaped into the car and started the engine. But where? Which way? At the junction ahead, how could he tell? He might be following them, might be losing them, while somewhere up there, all the time … At once he'd switched off the engine, sprung out and charged up the steep bank. But he'd had no torch and the moor above was a black, wet nightmare, slowly defeating him …

'They have taken mademoiselle, monsieur?'

Almost he was wishing they had: anything but what lights, daylight might reveal up there. Frénaye was shaking him.

'Monsieur, monsieur! We must think now what to do. Fear not but that the police will be sealing the roads, that these men will be cornered. We must make some plan!'

'And if she is dead?'

'Oh no, monsieur, no. As yet your thoughts cannot be clear. They have lost their hostage, their danger is acute, mademoiselle is the one card in their hand.'

'They may have shot her without thinking.'

'A woman unarmed? Why should they?'

'Then later, in anger ...'

'Oh monsieur no. If that, in the house you would have found her.' He went on shaking Gently. 'Listen, monsieur. These are men who plan, who calculate. They are not simple gangsters who shoot without purpose. At once their situation is plain and, without hesitating, they accept it. They have lost the game – they must think of their skins: they fly, and take a hostage with them.'

'She would not go willingly.'

'Oh monsieur, with a gun pressed in her back! Let us use the logic. Does she not know that monsieur will soon be on their tracks? The big prize is won, time now to be meek, to bend with the wind. She is a woman of keen intelligence. She will not lose the last trick for a gesture.'

The logic! If only it counted, could still the anguish of heart and brain. But for all the logic, in the black, black night that lay in a pall beyond the house ...

'In the house, any signs of violence, monsieur?'

'Broken windows. Stones.'

'Let us go in.'

Why not? He let Frénaye urge him towards the door.

The broken windows were upstairs. Below, the rooms were in perfect order. Except for dirty dishes, a stock of food, there were few traces of occupation. What did Frénaye expect? The inmates had brought themselves, had inhabited the house for forty-eight hours ... in the lounge there was a *Scotsman*, bought that morning, its principal news story the manhunt. Upstairs, Gently picked up a stone, stared at it, slipped it in his pocket ...

'Where have Guthrie's lot got to?'

'No doubt, monsieur, their first act will be to set up road blocks.'

'There could have been a siege going on out here.'

But the first patrol cars arrived only a few minutes later.

Guthrie himself was there quarter of an hour later: he could scarcely keep the glee from his porridgy face.

'My goodness man, this is a turn up! When it's over I must take that lassie's hand.'

'If that lassie is alive she's in deadly peril.'

'Ach man, never look on the black side. There's no sign yet that violence was offered, and if she's with them we'll fetch her off.'

'How long were you setting the road blocks?'

'Within minutes, man, of getting the call. I was fresh in, I'd just read your note. By now the whole barony is tight as a drum. Ach man, they're on the run – the job is sewn up – they've been stymied by one wee French lassie.'

'Has Empton been informed?'

Guthrie's look was sly. 'You know, I clean forgot to drop in and tell him ...'

Lights were working on the moor now, slowly criss-crossing, moving outwards. Moment by moment the situation was clarifying, reaching definition. She wasn't out there, must be alive. She'd been captured, dragged back to the house. The logic was sound; when they found they'd lost Barentin, they'd acted swiftly, knowing that time was against them. The brown Volvo had departed, turned left, reached the T-junction and made its decision, east or west: east to the A9 and its many feeders, west to Fort Augustus, the glens, Skye. Had it sprung the trap? Perhaps half-an-hour had elapsed before the first road block moved into position. By then the Volvo could have crossed the A9, be heading deep into country beyond. And McGash knew the country, that was evident: a third safe house was not improbable.

East: east was the quickest way out: west was a bottle-neck he might not clear ...

Guthrie was in his car getting flashes from control. There were blocks at Fort Augustus, Daviot, the town approaches. Cars were sifting the roads of the back country, calling in as they cleared their threads of the skein. Time moving on! Unless he'd gone to earth, McGash must surely have broken through the net. He wouldn't now be skulking about the back country roads, waiting for patrol cars to pick him up.

Gently got in beside Guthrie.

'Has Dalcross been alerted?'

'Surely he'd never head up that way!'

'He's got a hostage, may try to use her.'

Guthrie stared for a moment. 'You think he's clear, then?'

'I think he's made the A9,' Gently said. 'The other way we would have got him.'

'Blast,' Guthrie said. He grabbed the handset.

Men were coming in from the moor to stand aimlessly about the cars; Frénaye had retired to the Deux-Chevaux, where one caught the faint glow of his pipe. Suddenly meaning had drained out of that spot, out of the house, the operation; the house in particular was an empty shell, its broken windows insignificant. Gabrielle! With a handful of stones she'd solved the equation, set Barentin free. No guns, no grenades, no support: simply the sacrifice of herself. Barentin had been kind, at a terrible moment he had taken her into his protection, and now she'd paid the debt, substituting her life for his. Gabrielle ...! And he was left helpless: a gun at his side but no target.

'Where's Hénault?'

'We collected him,' Guthrie said. 'He'll be back at the station by now. Barentin I had a flash about. They've taken him to the Infirmary for a check up.'

'I'm going back to talk to Hénault.'

'Leave this one with me,' Guthrie said. 'I've got blocks now as far south as Aviemore and on the A's 95 and 96.'

'He knows the country,' Gently said.

'So do I,' Guthrie said. 'I've got it printed on my brain like a map.'

At Gently's approach Frénaye climbed from the Citroën.

'Monsieur, I fear that, for the moment, we have lost them ...'

'Take the Marina,' Gently said. 'Drive back to the police station. Wait for me in the yard.'

'The Marina ...?'

Gently handed him the keys. He himself got into the Citroën.

He let Frénaye precede him. The cramped cage of the Citroën brought back memories he hardly dared dwell on; yet he wanted it, the illusion of her presence, some moments alone in that precious car. It had a sweetish smell; not her scent, but the odour with which she must be familiar; and on the shelf were her maps, a purse, an open pack of Gauloise. He lit a Gauloise, and drove. Was it towards, or away, from her? Somehow he felt it was towards, though the feeling could not be supported by reason. Yet she was all round him: might it not be possible that here, in her car, some contact was being made: that an emotional radar was connecting him, pointing him, would lead him at last to her?

Gabrielle ...! In his anguish of spirit, for a while, he allowed himself to believe.

Frénaye was waiting patiently when he arrived at the police station carpark. Gently locked the Deux-Chevaux and together they entered reception. At the desk Gently asked:

'You have a prisoner Hénault?'

'He's in the cells, sir,' the desk sergeant said.

'Has Superintendent Empton seen him?'

The sergeant shook his head. 'The Super went out half-an-hour ago.'

'Went out where?'

'He didn't say, sir. One of his men came in and spoke to him. He just said to lock up the prisoner Petrie, then he was out of here in a hurry.'

Gently shrugged: so much the better! Perhaps he'd passed Empton on the road. Driving flat out, the Special Branch man would arrive at the scene just as others were leaving ...

'Bring Hénault to Superintendent Guthrie's office.'

A few minutes later the Frenchman was brought in. Now one could see he was a slim-built blond with small but well-formed features. And this was the man ...! Gently kept his stare neutral, pointed to a chair by the desk. Hénault sat. He had frank, grey eyes and on his lips hovered an appealing smile.

'You are Henri Hénault?'

'Monsieur.'

What had she seen in that male model's face? Presumably Hénault wasn't a homosexual, yet that was somewhat the impression he gave. The small mouth on which the smile sat gapped slightly to reveal even teeth.

'You are under arrest for illegal entry, conspiracy to kidnap and complicity in murder.'

The smile was wiped off; he jerked up straight.

'But ... monsieur ... that is scarcely fair! It is by my initiative entirely that Monsieur Barentin was rescued from assassins.'

'By your initiative?'

'At great risk monsieur, and in continual danger of my life. Also, I was drawn into this affair by a deception, and have myself been a prisoner throughout.'

'You were deceived into registering a false flight-plan?'

'Monsieur, I did not know that at the time.'

'Yet you flew to Scotland?'

'With a gun at my head! Would I have taken such risks of my own free will?'

Gently stared at him unforgivingly. The smile was still catching at the edge of his mouth. He had the air of a dog who is being reprimanded but who nevertheless is certain you don't really mean it. Things might happen but he wasn't quite responsible ... was this the trait she had found so fascinating?

'What precisely was your footing with McGash?'

'Monsieur, I was his prisoner and intended victim. He offered me much money, I pretended to believe him; in that way only could I stay alive.'

'He trusted you to buy provisions.'

'Oh monsieur, what a trust was that! While he is covering the shop with a gun. At no time was I in a position to escape.'

'Did he talk to you?'

'Of course.'

'Did he mention his plans?'

'But many times. When the deal is done we shall get a plane and I shall fly them out to Algiers. Then I shall be rich, I can go to Argentina and live it up with the *senoritas*.' Hénault shrugged expressively. 'But at Algiers airport two shots would have been the end of the business.'

'Did he name an airport at this end?'

'I am assuming it will be Inverness. When we arrived at that house he said now, it will not be so far to drive.'

'What were his contingency plans?'

Hénault looked vague. 'I think he is expecting to wait it out at the house. Because that area has already been searched he is confident that there he will be quite safe.'

Gently got up, took impatient steps. What he was fighting was the need for action! He couldn't accept that the traumatic emergency was beginning to lapse into a problem of strategy. Yet minute by minute that was what was happening, while phones didn't ring, road blocks failed: out there it was going on, but going on in a vacuum that defied every skill to pierce it.

'Describe McGash.'

He must have sounded fierce, because Hénault's incipient smile vanished. Frénaye, squatting by the window, was regarding him with mournful eyes.

'He – he is a violent man, monsieur.'

'You can tell me more than that.'

'He is – I think – perhaps a vain man, one who likes to be admired and thought a good fellow.'

'He liked you to admire him.'

'But yes. He wishes me to think him a great hero, one who has flair but at the same time is a complete professional. Of this he is proud, monsieur, that he is a professional first and last.'

'And the Arab?'

Hénault's mouth twitched. 'A killer, monsieur, exactly that. He says little, keeps to himself, but kills in a moment like a striking snake.'

'He killed the policeman.'

Hénault winced. 'He shot him directly the door opened. Then his dog – crack, crack! Two shots. The policeman died in great pain.'

'And McGash?'

'Didn't blink an eye monsieur. It was professional, it was done. Immediately we are in the car and on our way to the place prepared.'

'The Arab has no say.'

'But no. He is merely a shadow, a gun.'

'But loyal.'

'That is past question. McGash to that one is as God.'

Gently took more steps. 'Your ex-wife was captured.'

At first Hénault sat quite still. Then his hand went to his face and his shoulders trembled with silent sobbing.

'Stop that.'

'I cannot help it, monsieur! You do not know that woman. She is worth more than you or I together. And out of my cowardice I bring her to this.'

'She acted to save Barentin.'

'It was for me, monsieur, that she came. I begged her to come. I knew she would listen. Though I treated her badly, she would not forsake me.'

'Tonight the risk she took wasn't for you.'

'It is all the same, I am responsible. I cannot bear it, monsieur, I should have stayed. I might have killed one before they killed me '

'Listen Hénault. You know McGash. What is his reaction likely to be?'

'Monsieur, I dare not think—'

'I'm ordering you to think! In a crisis, would he stay rational?'

Hénault blubbered, swallowed, scrubbed hard at wet cheeks.

'I think – yes. He is a realist. But oh monsieur, something must be done.'

'He'd operate a plan.'

'Yes, a plan. He always knew what to do next.'

'And he talked. He talked plans to you.'

'But it is only what happens after—'

Gently grabbed his lapel. 'Think. Any names, dates you heard him drop.'

'Monsieur, there were none—'

'Any reference whatever to what might happen if things went wrong.'

'Monsieur – once – it is at the cottage – there he made some joke about Sutherland.'

'Sutherland!' Gently echoed.

'Yes, monsieur, but it was only in jest. The cottage was damp and unpleasant but at least, he said, it was better than Sutherland.'

Gently let go the lapel. 'And that's all?'

'I assure you, monsieur, it was a jest.' Hénault couldn't help dusting himself off. 'Monsieur, I cannot think he meant to go there.'

Sutherland: was it credible? On the wall of the office hung a map. Gently stared at it: it merely confirmed the improbability of such a notion. Fort Augustus, Inverness barred the way of the only two routes north. Sutherland was vast and empty, but McGash would scarcely be tempted to try for it.

The telephone on the desk clamoured. Gently picked it up: Guthrie.

'Man, we've just found the car.'

'What!'

'A brown Volvo abandoned by the docks. The dabs men are on their way to confirm it, but it can't be any other.'

Gently grabbed the phone hard. 'Could they have taken a boat?'

'Not quite so bad,' Guthrie said. 'It was left outside a compound used by oil men to park their cars when they're visiting rigs. The gate was forced. They'll have nicked a fresh car, and Christ knows when we'll find out what.'

'Then they've gone through the town.'

'Either that or they've doubled back this way to throw us off.' Guthrie sounded tired. 'But we've lost them for the moment. Now we don't even have a car to look for.'

'Anything in the Volvo?'

'Yeah,' Guthrie said. 'On the back seat, a leaf from a French pocket diary.'

'With writing?'

'No writing,' Guthrie said. 'Just to let us know.'

Gently hung up and sat silent for a time. In his corner, Frénaye drew on an empty pipe. Hénault looked as though he wanted to say something, but in the end kept his mouth shut. Finally Gently turned to him.

'She's still alive.'

'Oh monsieur, I am so glad,' Hénault said.

'But that's all,' Gently said. 'That's all.'

Hénault dropped his gaze and stared at his feet.

It was after midnight when Guthrie returned; he went straight to a drawer and got out bottle and glasses. Fatigue was showing in the drag of his mouth, the irritability of his motions. He was a large man, perhaps fifteen stone; had bowed shoulders, the beginnings of a paunch.

'Christ, I wish I could say something cheerful.'

He had gulped his first drink and poured a second. He sat leaning elbows on the desk, gazing at nothing as he sipped.

'I'm keeping the road blocks on, but McGash is far away now. I've ordered a general alert and special watch on ports and airfields. He's lost out. With any luck he'll dump the girl and go for cover. God, but I'm choked with this business – I've been flogging my men for three days.'

He drank; Gently drank. Outside the office were footsteps, voices. Then the thump of doors closing, the patter of a typewriter, ringing of a phone.

Gently said: 'Is Barentin guarded?'

Guthrie sighed, said: 'Two men. I looked in on him. He's still woozey. Otherwise the medic says he's ok. Gautier's there. He rang his embassy. The French still want it kept under wraps.'

'What happened to Empton,' Gently said.

'Yes, that's rather baffling,' Guthrie said. 'Tate's had a report in. Empton and his sidekicks have been down Glen Moriston, staking out a fruit farm.'

Gently sipped. 'A fruit farm?'

'Belongs to a laddie called McCrae,' Guthrie said. 'I'm told he was in here today delivering a load of raspberries to a supermarket. You may have seen him. He dined at your hotel. What would have sent Empton haring after him?'

Gently merely drank.

'Anyway,' Guthrie said. 'McCrae spotted the stake-out and rang us. Empton was last seen heading for town. Do you reckon Petrie fed him another dud line?'

'Possible,' Gently said.

'Yeah,' Guthrie said. 'That bastard's too clever, he'll cut himself. I couldn't help a smile.'

Gently didn't smile.

'Ach well,' Guthrie said. He poured more drinks.

Three hours since ... and everything done: nothing one could think of left undone. Guthrie was tired and needing his bed, had probably been whacked when he got back from Aviemore. What was he hoping for? Gently couldn't even think; simply that he couldn't let up, let go. Nothing left undone except to hang on, he here, she there, somehow together. That was it ...

The phone went. 'Thanks,' Guthrie said to it. Then the door opened and Empton walked in. He closed the door with a slam, strode into the room and stood glaring.

'Men at work,' he said. 'Men at work.'

He reversed a chair, straddled it, sat confronting them.

'Salute to the amateurs,' he said. 'And exit McGash to kill again.'

'Listen,' Guthrie said.

'No, you listen,' Empton said. 'Because you and Lucky Jim are going to answer for this. You withheld information, sent me off on a goose hunt and handed a free pass to a leading terrorist. Call it obstruction, call it bungling, but in my report I'll be calling it complicity.'

'Complicity!' Guthrie said.

'Complicity,' Empton said. 'You got off his hostage and let him go. You've been in communication with McGash, Lucky Jim's had a line to him from the start. Big deal, jock. But I'm the man with the brief, and that brief was to neutralize McGash. So don't think you can put in Barentin for bail, because Barentin isn't worth a plugged wollie.'

'By Jesus you'd better watch what you're saying,' Guthrie said.

'Had I old man?' Empton said. 'Don't think you'll be sitting for long in that chair after this little lot comes to light. I laid it on the line. Barentin was a zero. Barentin didn't count alive or dead. Our target was McGash, and McGash we could have had, but why didn't we? That's for you to answer.'

'Answer it!' Guthrie said. 'I'll answer it. To the Commission or whatever or wherever. And I'll answer you were after bloody murder, and not fit to be in charge.'

'Ha, ha,' Empton said. 'So funny. Take that line and your feet won't touch. The man who had McGash in a corner. The man who kissed him and waved him goodbye.'

'I've got a GA out,' Guthrie said. 'He can't get away.'

'Oh you lovely man,' Empton said. 'But a few hours ago you could have laid your hands on him, and what did you do then?' He turned to Gently. 'And you old man, Britain's answer to the Kremlin, when you knew where he was what did you do – apart from sending me to chase my tail?'

Gently stared and said nothing.

'He's strong, he's silent,' Empton said. 'Though not, apparently, an instant hero when it comes to facing Czech M52s. Better send in the girl friend, eh, old man? She's got some equipment that you lack. No doubt she's using it now to advantage. I daresay McGash can be quite a thrill.'

Gently rose. He picked Empton off the chair. He struck him in the stomach, then struck him in the face. Empton went down. He got up, sprang at Gently. Gently struck him again. Empton stayed down.

'You bastard!' Empton gasped. 'That was before witnesses.'

'What witnesses?' Guthrie said. 'I didn't see anything.'

'The Frog saw it!'

'Monsieur,' Frénaye said, 'by chance, I was looking out of this window.'

Empton went. They had another drink. Even the phones seemed to have fallen asleep. When finally Gently got back to his hotel room he searched it afresh; but there were no more bugs.

9

Guthrie had promised him immediate intelligence, but during the night Gently's phone stayed silent. He hadn't undressed, but lay dozing on the bed, snatching perhaps a couple of hours sleep. At seven he was wide awake. He stuffed his pipe, lit it, rang in. He got Tate.

'Give me a report.'

They had checked the Volvo, Tate told him; it had been stolen in Glasgow three weeks earlier, resprayed and given false plates. Dabs matched those at the cottage, the white house: one window was starred and a panel dented.

'What car did they take?'

'Nothing in yet, sir. The company are querying rigs and supply tenders. But these fellows get around, and its a funny old job to locate everyone who might have left a car there.'

'Possible sightings?'

'Sorry sir. We kept the blocks on till an hour ago.'

He smoked a while, went to stare through the window, then stripped and took his shower. Somehow he'd got to get an angle on it, find a way to come to grips with the problem. Hénault knew nothing. Petrie? Petrie had resisted Empton for hours, likely had no information beyond that of the safe house at Loch Ruthven. McGash might use him, but he wouldn't confide in him, wouldn't brief him except for his job. Unless there was a third safe house, Petrie was a dry well. Then? But the alternatives stopped there. One was left to stare at maps and pray for hunches.

He dressed and went down. He found Frénaye in the breakfast room. The Frenchman was also looking dull eyed; he glanced questioningly at Gently, who shrugged and shook his head.

'Monsieur, Empton has already gone out.'

Doubtless to try his luck with Hénault.

'Did he speak to you?'

'No monsieur. But he has most speaking looks.' Frénaye looked solemn. 'Monsieur, it remains essential that we are first to locate these terrorists. I fear that man. He is more determined than ever to have blood.'

'Any information will come to us first.'

'Monsieur, he is clever as well as barbaric. I fear that some aspect will occur to him that may not so readily occur to us.'

Gently frowned at the porridge just set before him. That indeed was the fear he couldn't dispel. Empton was good, he was on his own ground, if there was an angle he would spot it at once. Yet what? All night Gently had worried at it as he tossed on his sleepless bed. There was no angle: for him, for Empton, the problem was the same. And yet ...

'Eat up, and let's get over there.'

'Has monsieur a plan?'

'Just eat.'

Guthrie was closeted with Tate and another officer, an Inspector Black; after a few words he dismissed the latter and turned eagerly to Gently.

'I tried to ring you. That bastard Empton is across there with Hénault. He's doing his oily big brother act. Did you get anything from Hénault?'

'Only that McGash once mentioned Sutherland.'

'Sutherland,' Guthrie said. 'He's welcome to that. But nothing we can use?'

'If I had we'd be using it.'

'I suppose so,' Guthrie said. 'I just wondered. Myself, I've been having a chat with Petrie, but I'm pretty certain he knows nothing. As near as matters he let on that McGash was planning to sit it out at Loch Ruthven. So still we wait and hope. That sonofabitch must surface somewhere.'

'Sutherland was the name he dropped,' Gently said.

Guthrie shook his head. 'It doesn't make sense. Sutherland is a grand place to get lost in, but he'd never have dodged the blocks.'

'I think he might have done,' Gently said. 'If that was his aim. He beat the A9 block at Daviot. Then, after swopping vehicles, he could have filtered into town and perhaps outflanked the blocks.'

Still Guthrie shook his head. 'Too risky,' he said. 'He'd be asking for trouble if he came through here.'

'But if he took the risk,' Gently said, 'he'd be away, with open roads west and north.'

Guthrie pursed his lips. 'I think you're catching at straws, man, unless your information is better than you're saying. What was it McGash said about Sutherland?'

Gently hunched. 'Practically nothing.'

Tate said: 'I reckon he went east sir, and was down the A96 before we blocked it.'

'That's more likely,' Guthrie said. 'Heading for an exit, say Aberdeen. And if he does, we'll have him.'

Stalemate again: and time ticking on. Soon it would be twelve hours since the incident. And still she was out there, he was here, and all and nothing was done. Twelve hours: how had they been spent? What crises had been silently, obscuredly passing?

Guthrie rose. 'Sorry man, but I've got to get back to this job at Aviemore. Listen, as far as Tate is concerned you're in charge in my absence. Just give him the orders.'

Gently nodded.

'And I'll be praying for a break,' Guthrie said. 'But what you do is ok by me. If you take a chance I'll back it.'

He stuck out his hand, then left. Tate sought permission to return to his chores. After a spell, Gently sat down at the desk, lifted the phone and dialled.

'Gently. Give me Pagram.'

Down there at the Yard Pagram had probably only just come in. Gently's immediate senior in office, he had an agreeable distaste for red tape. He came to the phone.

'Hullo, hullo – is that the prodigal himself?'

'Never mind the comedy,' Gently said. 'Is the file on McGash still in the office?'

'If it isn't I can heist it,' Pagram said. 'But what's been going on up there old lad? We've had acrimonious dispatches from you-know-who asking for your hanging, drawing and quartering. What have you done to him?'

'Minor disagreements. Would you mind getting hold of that file?'

'It sounded more like war,' Pagram said. 'But not to worry, we still love you. What information is it you want?'

'Any connection between McGash and Sutherland.'

'Give me your number,' Pagram said. 'I'll check and ring back.'

Gently rested the phone. He lit his pipe. He encountered Frénaye's eye.

'Monsieur,' Frénaye said. 'This Sutherland, is it some place remote and wild?'

'That about describes it,' Gently puffed. 'Much of the interior is uninhabited.'

'It is, perhaps, somewhat like Corsica.'

'Perhaps somewhat,' Gently said. 'Add a few extra inches of rain and knock off several degrees centigrade.'

'Monsieur, I have visited Corsica,' Frénaye said. 'It is country very favourable to bandits and fugitives. If this McGash has reached such country it may not be easy to pick up his trail.'

Gently puffed and said nothing.

'Monsieur,' Frénaye said. 'Forgive my remarks.'

Gently smoked his pipe out: then the phone.

'Roger,' Pagram said. 'Here it is. On the record is an orienteering course that McGash took part in while he was at college. At Tongue.'

'At Tongue,' Gently said.

'No more and no less,' Pagram said. 'Is that the sound of a trained brain working like lightning?'

'Just harmonics,' Gently said. 'But thanks.'

He hung up, kept his hand on the phone. But wasn't this in truth clutching at straws? A dropped name, a cross-reference that, in his college days, McGash had visited the north coast! The one might well have given rise to the other, the memory of the visit supplying the remark. To make it credible one needed a third fix, something that tied it in beyond doubt. He raised the phone again.

'Connect me with Dornoch.'

After a delay he got a Superintendent Sinclair.

'Gently here. Can you give me a run down of incidents in your manor last night?'

'But—my stars!—is it yourself then?' Followed greetings, compliments, welcomes; then finally: 'Ach yes—there was one serious incident. I have an officer in dock following an attack.'

'A shooting?'

'Nothing of that sort, but a nasty business none the less. He must have caught some villains trying to steal petrol at a filling station by Bonar-Bridge. A truck driver spotted him lying there. He'd been struck on the head with something heavy.'

'Can he describe them?'

'Man, he's unconscious. They have him in intensive care.'

'When did it happen?'

'Three a.m. was when the truckie rang us.'

'Which side of Bonar?'

'The south. Man, do you think it's connected with your business?'

'Just a minute.'

Gently went to the wall map. Bonar-Bridge was sixty miles on from Inverness. There the road divided east and north ... and a fine ribbon through nowhere pointed up to Tongue. Had he enough? The time fitted if McGash had gone north after switching cars. Petrol he'd need, and a lonely filling station in the small hours was a likely resource. He went back to the phone.

'I'll be in your manor. There's a chance that McGash has headed your way.'

'Man, you can rely on me for support. Shall I see you at Dornoch?'

'Perhaps later,' Gently said.

He checked with Tate. Nothing fresh had come in; Empton was still in session with Hénault. Briefly he explained his decision to Tate, who listened with a cautious expression.

'Not much to go on, sir.'

It wasn't, but Gently didn't want to hear that.

'See that Guthrie is informed.'

'Yes sir. Will you be in touch?'

'When I can.'

Then, when they went to the car, it was Frénaye's turn to be doubting Thomas:

'Monsieur, I cannot help thinking that such attacks as you describe are unfortunately of common occurrence.'

'Get in,' Gently grunted. 'It's all we have.'

'But monsieur, the local police, knowing the ground ...'

'Are you with me or not?'

Looking slightly affronted Frénaye took his seat in the car.

He was right, because he had to be right: he had found a star and it wouldn't let him down. As soon as his wheels began turning north he could feel that sensation of the night before. He was driving towards her. Though now in the Marina, the signal was coming through clear. Ahead there, she was ahead: by yard and yard he was closing the gap. His facts might be few and his reasoning flimsy, but they were enough: he'd found the way.

Impatiently, he sat with traffic as they unravelled the Beauly Firth. Today, he noticed for the first time, was dry, though the sky was layered in grey. But the weather mattered nothing: just the direction. To be going north towards the grey hills. When the road left the Firth and offered straight stretches he began to overtake ambitiously.

'Monsieur,' Frénaye protested. 'Is our hurry so great?'

'Monsieur we have many miles to cover.'

'At the same time, monsieur,' Frénaye observed acidly, 'it is better to arrive with teeth than without.'

By eleven they had cleared Dingwall and then the traffic began to thin. Some moments of fragile sunlight were shimmering the low-shored Cromarty Firth. Ignoring the long loop of the A9, Gently struck inland on the A836, keeping the Marina booming across empty moor, under frowning rocks. This was the way they had come, he was convinced of it, during the black watches of the night: heading as straight north as they could get to Bonar and Sutherland beyond. But now how far ahead? In what obscure fastness of track and glen …?

Frénaye had been eyeing him uneasily.

'Monsieur, if these hopes should chance to be unfounded …'

'Monsieur, recall that in the area of search the single success was an empty car.'

'That, nevertheless, is a negative factor, pointing not one way or the other. For myself, I am enjoying the fine scenery, but without expectation of a miracle.'

'Monsieur, if miracles are needed, then miracles will be forthcoming.'

Frénaye shut up. They emerged at a summit to find Dornoch's angled firth at their feet. Mighty and luminous, it encircled far heights, a tiny train twinkling along the shore deep below. The road weaved its way down in coils. They picked up again with the A9. Bonar was signed: and a few minutes later the hoardings of a filling station appeared on the left.

Gently turned in. The filling-station was an old one: pumps, kiosk islanded in a stretch of rugged tarmac. Behind it squatted some low, neglected premises in concrete, containing however a toilet. Gently parked. A man came from the kiosk. He was short, middle-aged, dressed in dungarees.

'Police,' Gently said. 'Is this the filling station where an officer was attacked last night?'

'Aye,' the man said. 'This is it. So what's to do about it now?'

'Where were you?' Gently said.

'At home. The place is closed up at seven.'

'Had the pumps, the kiosk been interfered with?'

'No, just nothing at all,' the man said.

'Have you a self-service pump?'

'Yon at the end.'

'Was it used last night?'

'Aye, a few gallons.'

'Any English notes in the money put into it?'

'Aye,' the man said. 'But we see them often.'

Gently got out, walked to the pump, stood eyeing the spot where a car would have stood. On either side of the pump, oil stains, a few discarded wrappers, canister tabs. And something else. He picked it up. It was a scrap of paper with a torn edge. On the paper there was printing. What the printing said was: 'Lundi Decembre 25 – Noël'.

For a while he remained staring at the paper, then returned to the car and handed it to Frénaye. He leaned against the car. Frénaye examined the paper. The attendant stood by with curious eyes.

'Monsieur,' Frénaye said at last. 'I am lost for words. From this moment, monsieur, I hold your logic supreme. Where Maurice Frénaye contends for miracles, monsieur supplies them it seems at will.'

'They were here.'

'Past all doubt.'

'It was no comedy at the pumps that alerted that policeman.'

'Clearly, monsieur, she attracted his attention.'

'And, because of those houses, they couldn't risk a shot.' Gently clenched and unclenched his fists. He turned to the attendant. 'I'll use your phone.'

'Ach, but there's a pay phone—' the attendant began, but Gently brushed him aside and entered the kiosk.

'Get me Sinclair.'

Sinclair came on.

'I'm at the Bonar-Bridge filling-station,' Gently said. 'McGash was certainly here last night and it was he or his colleague who attacked your officer.'

'Jings, you don't say so!' Sinclair exclaimed.

'On my information he probably headed north. He is familiar with the Tongue district, may be seeking a hideout there.'

'Is that so,' Sinclair said. 'Then we'll have him. I'll put men in Tongue, Melness, Coldbackie. Aye, and I'll seal the coast road— and—and just whatever else you have in mind.'

'I'm going to follow up by the A836,' Gently said.

'Man, I'll give you a couple of cars.'

'You won't,' Gently said. 'These are dangerous men and they're holding a woman hostage. Leave the A836 to me. Keep your men at Tongue in low profile. If they spot McGash, no action, just observation until I get there.'

'Well, if you say so,' Sinclair said. 'But I'm thinking—'

'Play it as I say and stay clear. And advise Inverness for me.' Gently hesitated. 'Inspector Tate.'

'Aye, I ken Tate,' Sinclair said. 'But—'

'Make sure you speak to Tate in person.'

He hung up, placed a note on the counter, got back into the Marina. As he wheeled them once more on to the A9 the attendant came running, holding out change.

Across the bridge they entered Sutherland and rejoined the A836. A map open on his knees, Frénaye was checking the terrain ahead.

'Has monsieur a plan to communicate?'

'No plan,' Gently shrugged.

'We are coming to strange country, monsieur. To search such country would need many men.'

'With a car they can't stray far from the road.'

'But their car is not known to us,' Frénaye said.

'So,' Gently said. 'Any stationary car may be their car, will receive attention.'

He was still finding it difficult to suppress the emotion aroused by that little scrap of paper. So suddenly, lying in his hand, it had underwritten his reasoning, his belief. Till that moment he'd been nursing a long shot, driving himself by an act of faith: but now the long shot had become a certainty, made so by her intelligence, her opportunism. And must it not have been in her mind when she dropped that token that he it would be following, to catch at such trifles?

But Frénaye's common sense was right: the trail remained a tenuous trail. Though by extrapolation it pointed to Tongue a great blank existed in between. Also there were nagging alternatives. From Altnaharra a road departed along Strathnaver; and from this end the A837 diverged to Laxton Bridge and the north west. With twelve hours grace the odds were high that McGash had reached his destination, and then indeed it might take many men to flush him out.

They reached Lairg, an untidy settlement afflicted by hydro-electric workings. Here the double-track road ended and the A836 became a narrow lane. For a mile or two it skirted Loch Shin before turning again towards the north; then an RAC box appeared and by it the junction of the A837. Gently halted at the box.

'We'll search the verges.'

Frénaye took one direction, he the other. For a hundred yards they combed verges of fading heather, rock, mud. But this time there was nothing: perhaps in the darkness she hadn't noticed the junction, didn't realize its significance or wasn't able to make the drop.

'What now monsieur?'

'We keep going.'

So far, his luck hadn't let him down.

For a while they were driving across a plateau of sodden moor and plantations of pine, rimmed by dark hills and isolated peaks, some brightened by sun. Once or twice they passed hard-standings mauled by the tyres of forestry vehicles, but from these no tracks led and eventually they and the plantations ceased. It was like driving across the moon. Such vehicles as they met could be spotted from afar. Mostly it would be a truck or Land Rover; once a caravette with Australian markings. Meanwhile the hills, the peaks crept closer, showed sun-touched features through swirling mist; showers fell, sharp and sudden; sun spilled for a moment then was gone.

'Monsieur, a house ...'

Feature improbable! In fact it was the Crask Hotel. Possibly the loneliest habitation in Scotland, it marked a path to mournful Ben Klibreck. Gently pulled over, but the stop was a frost: McGash hadn't patronized the Crask Hotel. At the bar they bought canned beer and sandwiches before returning to the road.

'Monsieur,' Frénaye murmured. 'I speak it with regret, but I have fears that this task may be beyond us. Though the scenery continues superb, I find it fills me with misgiving.'

'Eat your sandwiches,' Gently grunted. 'If they came this way, they stuck to the road.'

Rain began falling steadily as the road climbed from the plateau to enter the hills. With hissing tyres and plugging wipers they drove the long, deserted stretches. A dismal road: the hills had a forlornness, a ruefulness of isolation; it was a place where few came and none stopped, a twilight land. Miles and time ticked up; since the Crask they had met not a single car. Finally came into sight a rain-dulled loch and the few sad houses of Altnaharra.

'Another hotel.'

But it yielded no more intelligence than its predecessor. At Altnaharra however information was vital to be had. Beyond the houses the Strathnaver road could be seen snaking away along the loch shore, while opposite it, Gently noticed with concern, another minor track departed. Three ways to choose from ... was it just possible for a miracle to happen again?

He pulled up beside a house, a hut in the garden of which was ambitiously signed: Post Office.

'Monsieur,' he said to Frénaye. 'We must search those verges. But first I wish to contact Superintendent Sinclair.'

'I will begin the search monsieur,' Frénaye assured him. 'By good fortune the rain has slackened.'

He set out for the junction, Gently for the hut. Inside it he found a simple counter; a smiling woman in an apron came forward to greet him in soft Scots. On a chance Gently showed her the photographs, but she merely shook her head. Then, having pushed the phone across the counter, she retired into the house. Gently rang.

'Sinclair? I'm at Altnaharra post office.'

'Is that so man?' Sinclair said. 'And have you anything to report?'

'Nothing,' Gently said. 'And you?'

'About the same,' Sinclair said. 'I've had reports from Tongue and the patrols, but no one's caught a glim of McGash. What'll we do?'

'Information,' Gently said. 'Have the roads been patrolled in this area today?'

'Aye,' Sinclair said. 'From Tongue to Altna' and up Strathnaver to Bettyhill. Then there'd be a rendezvous in Strathnaver with a patrol coming in from Helmsdale. But all's one, man, they've reported nothing. Either he was through there or still coming.'

'And – the third road?'

'Ach, that's a weary one, you will not find it on every map. I doubt if it sees a patrol more than once or twice a summer.'

'But it's driveable.'

'Aye, about. Are you thinking McGash may have gone that way?'

'I'm thinking it's possible,' Gently said. 'McGash has been orienteering in these parts.'

At Sinclair's end, a pause. 'I would not just be putting you off it,' he said. 'It's a driveable road – that's fair, though a trifle overgrown in places. But man it's lonesome. It runs up by Loch Hope and joins the coast road near Eriboll. That's to say it's going nowhere from nowhere, with nothing on the way but a Pictish fort. Let me put cars in.'

'No cars,' Gently said. 'But station a patrol at the other end.'

'Jings, but you're an obstinate laddie,' Sinclair said. 'Well, if that's your will, I'll do it.'

Gently said: 'Did you speak to Tate?'

'I spoke to him for quite a while,' Sinclair said.

Gently hung up and paid. Stepping from the hut, he saw Frénaye waving to him from a distance. The Frenchman came running:

'Monsieur – monsieur!'

In his hand he held a leaf from the little diary.

'Where did you find it?'

'Monsieur, along the road without a signpost.'

Gently half turned back towards the post office; then he shrugged.

'Let's go,' he said.

10

'Hand me the map.'

With engine running he glanced over the lie of the unposted road. Represented by hatched lines, it wound a way westward to turn north by Glen Golly. Then it passed under Ben Hope, one of two major peaks of the furthest north, before reaching the long finger of Loch Hope and connecting with the coast road where it left A'Mhoine. About twenty miles. A midway place name probably marked the Pictish broch; for the rest brown contours, burns and lochans signed in unpronounceable names. He gave the map to Frénaye and let in his clutch. Surely the trail was ending here! McGash could have chosen no retreat more favourable to his needs than the unposted road by Loch Hope.

The rain had eased but low cloud wrack clung to the strath and hills ahead. Narrow, bumpy and contorted, the little road defied any attempt to speed. The few roofs of Altnaharra were soon lost; a farm followed, reached by a track, then they were creeping along by a burn with gloomy heights peaking on their left. Grass grew along the centre of the road and heather bush encroached from the verges. It seemed a road that even Sutherland had surrendered, was tacitly allowing to vanish into history.

Yet:

'Monsieur, a vehicle has been along here. One is seeing broken twigs of heather.'

'But on both sides monsieur – a wide vehicle, perhaps the Land Rover of a farmer.'

'Monsieur, it may be that McGash has a Land Rover. For this country such a vehicle would be a wise choice.'

'In that case, monsieur, we must double our vigilance, since McGash will not be restricted to the road.'

A worrying thought. With four-wheel drive McGash could truly take off into nowhere: into the wilds of Glen Golly, for example, which his previous visit may have made known to him.

'Monsieur,' Frénaye said. 'He will still need food.'

'He could have stocked up,' Gently said.

'It would have occasioned him delay, monsieur. I do not think he waited for a shop to open.'

But they were dealing with a planner. If McGash had known his goal he would have taken steps to provide what was necessary: not waiting patiently for shutters to come down, but going in with a brick or a jemmy. Perhaps even now the store at Lairg was counting the cost and ringing their insurance ...

'Watch for signs of a vehicle having left the road.'

'I will do so,' Frénaye said.

The smudge of a road was slowly climbing, fretting its way into hills. To the north they could see the high hump of Ben Hope appearing and disappearing in wrack. Then they rumbled over a primitive bridge to open a prospect of Glen Golly. Gently halted, got out and went to make an inspection of the approaches.

No tracks. He put glasses on the glen. At the far end rose a peak of ghostly white. Presumably cased in quartzite, it appeared to have been whitewashed in some ancient freak and then abandoned to weather. The glen itself was smoking with mist, a wide strath hemmed by peaks. Mentally Gently tossed a coin, shrugged and got back in the car.

So on again, with the neglected surface bringing out the worst in the Marina's suspension. Now they were tracking beside a rock-strewn river that rambled capriciously, a hundred feet below. Ashes, alders, hazels tufted its banks; here and there trees clung to the roadside. Ahead the high walls of Ben Hope were beginning to press closer, as though barring access. Then suddenly, like a giant potsherd, the ruin of the broch appeared before them, occupying a natural platform above the river; and parked beside it, a motor caravan.

'Monsieur ...!'

His reactions were too slow. For a moment the motor caravan had merely surprised him: a vehicle so unexpected, so seemingly innocent, standing apparently deserted by the uncouth ruin. Then he braked furiously, snatched at reverse. Above the rev of the engine he heard a scream. Instantly the screen shattered and something white hot seared his cheek. The car lurched backwards. Hammers struck it: the nearside tyre exploded. The car wobbled backwards a few yards, dropped a wheel over the verge, stopped.

'Out ...!'

He sprawled through his door, raced round the car and dived for cover. A few yards away Frénaye crashed down the bank, rolled himself into the cover of hazels. They tugged out guns. Moments later came the sound of slammed doors, an engine firing. With a cry Frénaye broke cover and scrambled back up the bank.

'Stay down!' Gently snarled, but Frénaye ignored him. Swearing, Gently scrambled up too. He was just in time to strike Frénaye's gun aside as the Frenchman aimed after the departing motor caravan.

'Monsieur – I can hit a tyre—!'

'Monsieur, in that vehicle is an innocent person.'

'But we cannot let them go.'

'We shall let them go. At the end of this road the police have a trap.'

'But monsieur, will the police recognize them? I saw a man who was not like the one in the picture.'

'What!'

'But no,' Frénaye said. 'This one is clean-shaven and wears shoulder-length hair.'

'Let's get this car back on the road.'

The poor Marina looked a mess. Besides the burst tyre and shattered screen steam was coming from a punctured radiator. Together they heaved it on an even keel and Gently raised the bonnet lid: a bullet had penetrated the top of the radiator and buried itself in the air filter.

'We can plug it – but we'll need water.'

'I can fetch some in the beer cans, monsieur.'

Frénaye charged off down to the river while Gently cut plugs from a hazel and hammered them home. Then a wheel change: by chance the spare tyre was soft as a sausage. Finally, using the jack handle, Gently got rid of the fragments of the screen.

'Now ... if she'll start.'

The Marina started; but the affair had lost them twenty-five minutes. By now, even at the speed the road imposed, the motor caravan would be half a dozen miles ahead. McGash had changed appearance, that was certain; at the least he had shaved and donned a wig; and that, along with the unlikely vehicle he was driving, might well get him by the lurking patrol car.

'Ah monsieur, if we could find a telephone!'

'The nearest phone is at Altnaharra.'

'Would it not perhaps be better to turn about?'

Gently set his mouth tight and trundled on.

Straight after the ruined broch they had sighted another building, but this also was ruinous, an unroofed shieling. Then the steep side of Ben Hope closed in and they were gnawing along at its foot. Draughty, with glass crunching under heel, the Marina was likewise beginning to overheat: the odds were that they wouldn't reach the coast road. Already, the engine sounded lumpy.

'Monsieur ... we come to a lake.'

They had struggled on to the toe of Loch Hope. Cursing silently, Gently stopped the car and Frénaye scrambled through scrub to fill the beer cans. To have been so near, and still to lose out! Her scream was still sounding in his ear. A scream of warning. Had she seen who it was, knew now that her desperate trail had not been in vain? He felt suddenly near to tears. What had been her reward for that reckless cry?

They poured water into the hissing radiator, climbed back in and limped off again. Having reached the loch shore the road levelled out to pace along it in short, grass-choked stretches. Another five miles? Six? One glimpsed the grey water progressing endlessly. On the far shore, a dismal low strath backed by low, featureless hills. A single bright spot: McGash had been flushed and could no longer lie low in this desolate sector. He would have to think again: and his first move now must be to get rid of the identified van ...

And Gabrielle?

If McGash's motive was to vanish, Gabrielle could only be a nuisance to him: a useless hostage. How would he deal with it? To give himself time ... maximize his chances?

'Monsieur – halt, halt!'

This time he was quicker – in fact they both ducked towards the gap above the dash! Surmounting a switchback they had brought into view an extended reach of the loch shore. Also a house, old, weathered, with boards nailed to several of its windows: also – parked before it, with doors yawning wide – the van that should have been many miles away.

'Let's get out of sight!'

He sent the car down the switchback until the house and the van disappeared behind trees. Then he lammed the car as far as it would go into an overgrown remnant of passing-place.

'Can they have run short of petrol, monsieur?'

Gently shook his head. 'Unlike McGash.'

'Then that house is perhaps his hideout?'

'If that was the idea it's busted now.'

Seizing glasses, he hurried back up the slope, with Frénaye close behind. An apron of grey sandstone made a lookout from which he could study the house unseen. A house too evidently abandoned; plaster was slipping from rough stone walls; the garden was a tangle of grass in which, however, a few flowers still struggled. No movement. All the van doors were open, as though the occupants had left in haste. A big timber wood shed was built on to the house and, down at the shore, one could see a boat shelter.

'Take a look.'

He gave Frénaye the glasses, himself studied the lie of the land. Trees, mainly oak and ash, formed cover almost up to the garden fence. Beyond the house was a heathery knoll, across the road opposite moor and scrub: a nearer approach was possible ... but where were McGash and colleague?

'Monsieur, I have a feeling that our caution is superfluous.'

'I can't see McGash taking off on foot,' Gently said.

'Monsieur, he would wish to change vehicles, and here he may have stumbled on an opportunity.'

'A car – down there?'

'It is possible. The property, though old, may be sometimes visited. The van would appear to have been unloaded, and I observe no sign of any persons.'

Gently brooded: the explanation was credible. That house could no longer represent a hideout. Yet if McGash had indeed swopped vehicles, would he not have taken pains to conceal the van? It could well have been hidden behind the house – had he really been in such a hurry? And ... if the explanation was correct ... what were they going to find down there?

Something was wrong. The boarded house, the abandoned van had a sinister air ...

'We'll approach from cover.'

'Very good monsieur.'

They went back down the road and past the car. A gap gave them entry to the trees, among which bush hazel grew thickly. They approached the fence.

'Guns.'

He sent Frénaye wide, crept forward to observe. Still no movement, no sound: the van stood only twenty yards from the fence.

'Cover me.'

He rose quickly, jumped the fence, ran fast for the van. Nothing happened. The van was quite empty. The house stayed silent, blind windowed, still.

'Come ...'

Frénaye joined him. Like Gently, he peered into the van.

'What do you make of it?'

Frénaye's shoulders moved. 'Precisely what I did before monsieur. They have secured a fresh vehicle.'

'So where is the driver?'

'Is it not possible they took him with them?'

'Why do that?'

'To render him harmless.'

'McGash has quicker ways of doing it.'

'In that case monsieur—' Frénaye was beginning, when a sudden clamour jerked them about. It came from the wood shed: someone appeared to be hammering on the door with a heavy instrument. Then a muffled voice cried out:

'Messieurs ... messieurs ... I am a prisoner!'

'Gabrielle!' Gently exclaimed.

At once they were pounding over the tangled grass. The wood shed door, heavy, paintless, was secured by a hasp in which a peg had been jammed.

'Gabrielle!'

'Oh Monsieur George!'

He threw down his gun to struggle with the hasp. The peg was wet and swollen: Frénaye grabbed a nugget of rock and handed it to him.

'Oh monsieur – please be quick!'

'A moment!' Gently cried.

'Take your time, laddie,' a voice said behind him. 'You'll be in there with her before you can blink.'

Gently swung round. He was staring at the clean-shaven, long-haired man of Frénaye's description. In his hand the man held a Czech M52: a door at the end of the house stood ajar.

'Drop that rock.'

Slowly, Gently let it fall. Frénaye's hands were already clutching air. A black haired, narrow-faced man stood beside Frénaye. He'd come round the wood shed. He also held an M52.

The long-haired man motioned with his gun.

'Flat on the ground, the pair of you.'

There was nothing for it; they got down and stretched out on the wet grass.

'Frisk them, Dusty.'

Busy fingers explored them, collecting their wallets, a knife of Frénaye's. The long-haired man took them, jammed them in his pocket. From the wood shed came no sound.

'Up and through that door.'

Dusty backed in first behind his gun. They entered a dank, dark room, a kitchen, still with a few sticks of furniture. The window was blocked; there were two inner doors, one of which would give access to the wood shed. Sunk into a wall was a big kitchen range where rust and black lead contended.

'Sit over there – on the floor.'

They sat down on grubby concrete. Dusty lounged by them with his gun. The long-haired man took out the wallets, went through them, tossed them down on a table. He sat.

'So you're Gently.'

'And you're McGash,' Gently said.

They stared at each other. McGash had smoky grey eyes, broad features, a heavy chin. The eyes were deep set, narrowed. He had a thin-lipped, straight-lined mouth. He looked strong, had deep shoulders; he was dressed in blue jeans.

The Arab Yousef was of slighter, more wiry build and had a glitter in his coal black eyes. His gun was very solid in his hand. He wore a bomber-jacket over black jean slacks.

'Gently,' McGash said. 'I'm getting lucky. I hadn't hoped for the likes of you, man.' He laughed suddenly. 'I'm telling you, laddie, this opens up new lines of thought.'

'So you can let the girl go,' Gently said.

'Can I now,' McGash said. 'And what's she to you?'

'She's nobody,' Gently said. 'A useless hostage. You'll have to make a deal now, and the girl's no part of it.'

'Listen to him telling me,' McGash said. 'You're in no position to talk deals, Geordie.'

'You'll have to deal.'

'And what for should I, when I can clean the slate and be on my way?' He laughed again. 'Don't kid yourself, Geordie. If you're a professional, so am I. And I will not be turning a hair, man, when I'm squaring accounts with the like of you.'

'Without a hostage, McGash, you're dead meat.'

'Just hear who's talking,' McGash said.

'Cartier shot Starnberg,' Gently said. 'But there's a man bloodier than Cartier coming this way. He wants you dead, not alive, and if you don't make a deal now dead is what you will be.'

McGash waved the hump-backed automatic at him. 'And you'd be for taking me alive?' he said.

'Preferably alive.'

'Then you're no bloody professional – whatever they reckon to you in London.'

'And you,' Gently said. 'You're such a professional?'

'Don't chance it with me, man,' McGash said.

'You go for the big one – snatch Barentin – and let a pair of amateurs take him off you?'

'Geordie, I'm warning you,' McGash said.

'A fine professional,' Gently said. 'You trusted Hénault, let him get to a phone, and the third time set it up. A girl took you. A child could have done it. All your brains are in what you're holding. You're a professional gunman McGash – take your weapon, and where are you?'

McGash jumped up; his face was working. He held the gun at Gently's head. The gun was trembling. For moments he stood there. The Arab was watching him with bright eyes. Then McGash struck a blow with the muzzle of the gun that set blood trickling down Gently's cheek.

'You London bastard – you thought I'd fall for it!'

Gently held his hand to his face.

Shaking slightly, McGash backed to the chair. He held the gun on Gently with both hands.

'You'd better say your prayers, you bastard.'

'McGash, this road is sealed at both ends.'

'They'll find a dead copper.'

'You can't get out. Either you deal or you're finished.'

'But first I settle with you, Geordie.'

'Let the girl take your terms.'

McGash half rose again from the chair. 'Stop bloody telling me what to do!'

He dumped down hard, sat glaring at Gently. Still the gun pointed at Gently's head. Hajjar said something to McGash in Arabic: McGash snapped back in the same language. Frénaye was sitting with one leg drawn up, his hands pressed hard against the wall behind him.

'You're a clever boy,' McGash said.

Gently went on nursing his cheek.

'I'm going to kill you,' McGash said. 'Don't kid yourself, Geordie. You're just alive till I feel like pressing this trigger. I'd have killed you anyway, for Starnberg. But now killing you will be a pleasure. And you won't know when, Geordie, you're living by the minute. Any time at all I could be pulling this trigger.'

'Like a gunman,' Gently said. 'Did they teach you nothing?'

'This minute,' McGash said. 'Or the next. So I've lost Barentin, the man says, but who have I got now waiting for a bullet?'

Gently nursed his cheek.

'But,' McGash said, 'when I'm ready. No bastard from London teaches me my job. I can use you, Geordie, but that's my affair, and don't think it will get you off the hook.'

'Why not ask Yousef?' Gently said. 'He isn't in it just for the cash.'

'You can forget Yousef,' McGash said. 'He likes killing. He can't wait.'

'But at least,' Gently said, 'he's killing in a cause, has got people back there he thinks he's serving. That makes him different from a hired gun sweating on loot in an Aden bank.'

The M52 was trembling again.

'You'll talk yourself dead,' McGash said.

Gently hunched, stared at him, flicked a little blood from his face.

'Monsieur, with respect,' Frénaye said. 'Is the money indeed not intended for yourself?'

'Belt-up Frog!' McGash snapped. 'You're nothing, and you'll soon be less.'

'I cannot help enquiring, monsieur,' Frénaye said, 'when you take such risks at other people's bidding. No doubt their gratitude will be profound, but may it not extend to a share of the takings?'

For an instant McGash's gun swung to Frénaye, and Gently tensed himself for a jump. Then he caught the Arab's glittering eye. McGash's gun swung back.

'I don't have to spell it out for you crap.'

'If monsieur feels the issue is too sensitive ...'

'Listen,' McGash said, 'you're dead ducks, both of you, there's ways of killing you wouldn't believe. Just pray I'm in a hurry, just pray for that. You'll find I know how to do what I'm paid for.'

'What you're paid for,' Gently said. 'Hired, paid.'

'So who isn't paid,' McGash said. 'What are you paid for?'

'You kill, take your pay,' Gently said. 'And pray that other men aren't like you.'

McGash was breathing hard. His sunken eyes were jacked wide; the thin mouth hung open, showing teeth. He stared first at one, then the other: the muzzle of the M52 was wavering.

'You bastard,' he said. 'You bastard. What I'm doing is a political thing.

'Not you,' Gently said. 'You're criminal. Politics end where crime begins.'

'I'm political,' McGash said. 'My bloody crimes are political.'

'Just bloody,' Gently said. 'You can't have it both ways. A murderer for Christ is still a murderer, no longer a hero, no longer a politician.'

'Tell the wogs that,' McGash said. 'Where I come from they call me a hero.'

'And you can believe them?' Gently said. 'You can worship your image, wish society was made up of such men as you?'

'It would be free,' McGash said. 'A free society.'

'Just the jungle,' Gently said.

'I'm bloody telling you,' McGash said. 'Bloody telling you.'

Gently dabbed his cheek, said nothing.

'Monsieur,' Frénaye said. 'In this there is truth, that society coheres because of honest men.'

McGash glared furiously at him, but the gun was level again in his hand. All this time the Arab had lounged nonchalantly, perhaps unable to follow the English. Once, beyond the door to the wood shed, there had been a faint scuffle, as though someone had stumbled over a solid object. Then silence. The door was substantial, secured top and bottom by rusty bolts.

'You haven't too much time McGash,' Gently said.

'If you want to die,' McGash said. 'Open your trap once more. I'm not taking it, Geordie, I've heard enough. I'll be shutting you up one way or another.'

'Then you're finished.'

'Shut your trap!'

'If you kill me you kill yourself,' Gently said. 'You won't be tucked up in a security prison waiting for some of your colleagues to spring you. That's out. Get rid of me, and you'll be cut down like a dog.'

'After you, Geordie, there's two to go.'

'You're not reading me, McGash,' Gently said. 'I'm a card you've got to play now, because a few hours more will be too late. There's a man who's sworn to have you. He doesn't give a damn for any hostage. You could have had Barentin on the end of a gun and he'd have blasted you just the same. Either you deal now or you're dead, and I'm the only trump in your hand.'

McGash stared with narrowed eyes. 'Is that so, Geordie?' he said. 'And who might he be, this bold chiel, who'll come hunting for a quick bullet?'

'Never mind his name,' Gently said. 'I've been holding him off you, McGash. I'm still holding him off you, but it can't be for long now. You're trapped. The local police know I'm here. Soon they'll be sending in men. And then he'll come, and the shooting will start, and whoever lives you're going to die.'

'You're bluffing,' McGash said.

'Don't make that mistake.'

'I'm thinking you're a cunning devil,' McGash said.

'What you've got to do, and do quickly, is to send the girl out with your terms.'

'Aye, to bring in your bogeyman!' McGash said savagely.

'There's still time to deal with the local police.'

'And I'm saying it's trickery.'

Gently shrugged, dabbed again at his bloody cheek.

McGash sat gazing for a while, then snapped a remark at Hajjar. There was a rapid interchange between them, at times almost an argument. Finally the Arab nodded once or twice and gestured with lean shoulders. Never once had his eyes moved from the two men seated on the floor.

'Right,' McGash said. 'So where's your car, Geordie?'

'Up the road,' Gently said. 'Partly disabled.'

'It fetched you here,' McGash said. 'It'll do. It'll take a man on to the junction.'

'A man,' Gently said.

McGash laughed unpleasantly. 'Did you think I'd be jumping to your orders, Geordie? Man, I'd sooner trust a nest of scorpions. It's the Frog who'll be carrying the terms.'

'Let the girl go,' Gently said. 'She's taken enough.'

'I'm telling you,' McGash said. 'There's a score to settle there.'

'Let her go. If you want them to listen.'

'They'll listen,' McGash said. 'Oh yes, they'll listen.' He rose. 'On your face, Geordie boy.'

Gently stared at him, then obeyed.

'Up, you,' McGash said to Frénaye. 'And don't waste your time trying to jump Dusty.'

Frénaye left with the Arab. Time passed; then one heard the Marina's engine. It cut. Frénaye returned, his hand to an angry welt on his jaw.

'Don't say I didn't warn you,' McGash said.

'Monsieur, the radiator must be filled with water.'

'So down beside Geordie,' McGash said. 'We'll let Dusty take care of that.'

The radiator was filled.

'Now Froggie,' McGash said. 'This is what you'll be telling the police. I'm wanting a car with a full tank, an escort, and a plane standing by at Wick airport. I'm wanting them now.' He looked at his watch. 'At six p.m. I'll be shooting a hostage. Are you hearing me, Froggie?'

'Clearly monsieur,' Frénaye said. 'At six p.m. you are shooting a hostage.'

'Don't forget that,' McGash said. 'Whatever else. And here's the rest of the message, Froggie. The money agreed is to be paid over, and deposit confirmed at Algiers airport.'

'A hostage to be shot,' Frénaye said. 'And money paid over.'

'You've learned your lesson,' McGash said. 'Now on your way. And listen, Froggie – you're the lucky one. Show your face here again and you'll stop a bullet.'

'Monsieur ...?' Frénaye said to Gently.

'Do it,' Gently said. 'Inform Superintendent Sinclair.'

'Monsieur,' Frénaye said. 'I shall do my best.'

'Up,' McGash said. 'You'll do just what you're told.'

The Marina drove off and Yousef returned.

'Let's see your face, Geordie,' McGash said. 'My, that's a nasty cut, I'm thinking it could use a couple of stitches.'

Gently said nothing.

'You're quiet man,' McGash said. 'Where are all those fine words you were dinning in my lugs?'

'That man is too dumb, I think,' the Arab said. 'Perhaps I am loosening his tongue, just a little?'

'Ach no,' McGash said. 'That's nasty. It's a bullet or nothing for a man like Geordie.' He laughed. 'He's a man of compassion, that's what Geordie boy is. I'm thinking he'll like to break the news to the girl that she's for the chop in a couple of hours.'

Gently said nothing.

'Open the door,' McGash said. 'I've had a gutful of his ugly face.'

Yousef shot the bolts of the door to the wood shed; they kicked him through it, into darkness.

11

The floor of the wood shed was at a lower level than the floor of the kitchen. Gently stumbled forward and sprawled headlong into a great pile of wood chumps. The door slammed and was bolted. Light now came only through cracks; the darkness was charged with the sweet smell of sawn pine. He sensed movement near him.

'Monsieur ...? George ...?'

'Gabrielle ...!'

What motion of theirs was it that brought them together? He could never decide: just that suddenly they were clasped as one, scarcely able to breathe. And at the same moment the situation became one of pure fantasy: it was laughable: the darkness was sun: the people beyond the door mouthing puppets. Perhaps that was why she was crying, why he was crying too.

'George ...!'

'Gabrielle ...!'

'George ...!'

What else in the universe was there to say? Well, something else. After a while she found out what it was.

'George ... I'm in such a mess.'

As if that could matter, ever.

'I haven't washed ...'

'Don't be stupid.'

'I'm sure I smell—'

He simply kissed her.

'Ahhh! Then you still love me?'

How could she be so absurd? The word was a meaningless label that had ceased to apply to their condition. To love there must be two: in that moment they had gone beyond it. Yet, there must be words.

'Are you all right?'

'Those pigs have knocked me about ... and I'm filthy!'

'Nothing else ...?'

'Oh … no. Didn't you know? Those bastards are queers.' She gave a little laugh that was almost a sob.

'Are you much hurt?'

'Just bruises. And a black eye, if you could see it. But you?'

'Only a scratch.'

'Oh my dear.' She hugged him to her

'Gabrielle, why did you do it?'

'Ha! It was not for that blackguard Henri. You do not think that?'

'I could have rescued Barentin, probably had that pair behind bars.'

'George, I had to do it myself.'

'Gabrielle, it was a rash gesture.'

'Oh my dear, you do not understand. I had to do it before … before …' She hid her face against his chest.

'Not for me.'

'Oh yes … oh yes. For you. To cleanse myself of so much. How else could I come to you, I who betrayed you in my acts, in my heart?'

'You did none of these things.'

'But yes. Till this very moment I am betraying you. Back there at the ruin, when we heard your car coming, I could not conceal from them my feelings. So they set an ambush. Then again here I am the foolish bait for their trap. I believed them when they said they were leaving me and, when I heard you, called out. After these things, how can you love me?'

'These things are nothing.'

'To me, how much!'

'Between us there can be no debts.

'Oh George, hate me, but do not cease to love.'

She sobbed for a time. His eyes were slowly adjusting to the darkness. He could see she was wearing a soiled anorak, sweater, muddy slacks. He turned her face up to his. Her cheeks were smeared with dirt and tears. One eye was black and almost closed. Very softly he kissed it.

'A brave girl.'

'Those pigs. Oh George, I'm ugly.'

'Only beautiful.'

'This isn't the way that I was planning it at all. I wanted to be fresh from a bath, all scented and seductive. I wished to destroy you with my body, my friend, till there was nothing you would not forgive me. Do you not recall our private room at Honfleur?'

'I recall our private room.'

'That evening, my friend, I bathed like some mad woman and used every aid in my repertoire. Yet I was not late?'

'You were waiting for me.'

'I feared that my haste would bring on a sweat. In that lounge bar I was on pins to get you away to our room. Was I not beautiful then?'

'Beautiful then, more beautiful now.'

'Ha, do not flatter, my friend.'

'I do not flatter,' Gently said.

She turned away. 'I have been in that corner and I had nothing with which to wipe. And am I still beautiful?'

'You are still beautiful.'

'Oh my friend. Love me, love me!'

Through the door, dulled sounds of movements, occasional unintelligible exchanges. Other than the heap of chumps the wood shed contained nothing but some empty shelves. Wouldn't there have been an axe? Probably removed. The chumps were old, had bark that was peeling. Walls, roof were of solid planks fastened to hefty framing and rafters.

Gabrielle shuddered. 'My love, I was listening. I heard what was said behind that door.'

'Bluff,' Gently said. 'McGash wouldn't dare do it. He's been in these situations before.'

'Beloved ... if I must ... I think I can die.'

'Listen to me,' Gently said. He held her from him. 'If McGash loses you, he's left only with me, and I'm his passport to Algiers and the cash. Then he'll be in a situation of stalemate and the police will only have to wait him out. So he can threaten, but that's all. If he loses you, he loses the game.'

'But ... if he still has you?'

'He can't use me. I have to stay alive until Algiers. The police will know that threats against me are empty and they will simply sit tight. With you, he hopes to win a battle of nerves, but if his bluff is called he's lost.'

She shuddered afresh. 'It is logical, but ...'

'Unfortunately there is another factor.'

'How—?'

He told her about Empton. She listened, leaning heavy in his arms.

'He will not care if we die?'

'He will not care.'

'Look at me, my love,' Gabrielle said. 'It is worth it. I have died once already. To die now in your arms will be for me a great happiness.'

'There will be no dying,' Gently said. 'McGash doesn't want to die. He knows now that his bluff must succeed quickly or he will have to surrender to Sinclair. And Sinclair's no mug. He'll see through the bluff, keep stringing McGash along. And in the end McGash will break and go for the better option.'

'My friend, that man enjoys killing.'

'He also enjoys living,' Gently said.

'Yet, in a moment of exasperation—'

'He's sitting in there now,' Gently said, 'weighing his chances.'

Gabrielle sighed. 'You are a great man,' she said. 'I will believe what you believe. Yet is there not some action we can take, my friend, to make your logic still more strong?'

Gently hunched. 'We have a stack of blunt instruments.'

'And if I, by screaming, could make them open that door?'

Gently thought about it, slowly he shook his head. 'It wouldn't fool me, wouldn't fool McGash.'

'But we could try it?'

'I could only take one of them.'

'I, my friend, could take the other.'

Gently shook his head decidedly. 'No. We too must go for a better option.'

'Then ... can we not escape?'

'You stay here.'

Cautiously he rose, picked his way to the outer door. He put his weight against it. It creaked faintly but gave scarcely at all. The hasp he knew was of heavy construction and there was no prospect of shaking out the peg. Hinges were concealed between door and jamb. The frame was rebated, making leverage difficult. Not that way. He proceeded to the walls. The planks of the cladding were damp and tight. He tested one with the pressure of his foot. No give. To get out of the wood shed one needed that axe ...

He looked for it, but there was no axe, and in any case no

prospect of its silent employment. He explored the rest of the shed. He found nothing but rusty tins.

'We cannot get out?'

'No.'

'Will the police be very long, my friend?'

'If the car kept going they will be here shortly. But nothing will happen until Sinclair arrives.'

'Then, my love, let us employ the interval as though none of this were happening at all. I have been out of your arms now for five minutes, and I do not like the sensation.'

He sat down again on the chumps, took her in his arms and kissed her. The kiss was interrupted by creaking sounds from behind the door, then a tinkling of glass. She sat up straight.

'What are they doing?'

'Probably removing a board from the window,' Gently said. 'McGash is setting the scene.'

'Then I wish, my love, he would do it more quietly.'

They listened. More glass tinkled; there were movements, words, then quiet again. At last she snuggled back in his arms, pulled his head down, completed the kiss.

'Beloved, I remember many things.'

'I remember many things too.'

'When you knew what must happen, but I did not, on the phone you told me to remember that you loved me.'

'I could not tell you more.'

'Oh my love it was too much. I remembered it and felt I could not live. To have had it and then not to have it was a desolation too great to bear. It was in my brain when I walked by the harbour. I could think of only one way to pluck it out.'

'You have never not had it.'

'But how could I believe that.'

'Once we had loved it could never change.'

'Then my dear I was an infidel in my love, my faith for a while was lost in madness. But still in my brain as I lost consciousness I heard your words like a summons.'

'I was distraught. I sought you everywhere.'

'My love, I was mad indeed. I had lost faith, I dared not meet you. Scorn in your eye would have killed me afresh.'

'Yesterday I followed you from Invergarry. When you watched I was watching you.'

'Then it is true. I felt nowhere alone. As though everywhere a hand was on my arm.'

'Again today I knew where to look for you.'

'Again today I knew you were following. My love, there can be no death for us. It is all but the beginning of new eternities.'

'First, I mean to live out the old one.'

'And shall that be in your land or mine?'

'In both our lands. For us, the Channel will become a private highway.'

She gave a deep sigh. 'Ah, my love! Will you deny now that love has its miracles? Kiss me and hold me close. Though men may kill they cannot kill this.'

He kissed her. From next door there was silence. Could they have been listening to this breathed conversation? Not the slightest sound was penetrating to their dark, wood-scented hush. But then, after moments, he heard the van doors slammed, the engine started, the van driven from the frontage. More preparations: the van had offered cover, might have let in marksmen to within yards of the house. Gabrielle's head lifted.

'They have not gone, my friend ...?'

'No,' Gently said. 'They haven't gone.'

'I would not mind being left here with you. The police could find us later, some day, never.'

'Shortly the police will be here.'

'Then I think it is too soon.'

'Keep your voice low.'

She gave a tiny wriggle and resettled her head on his chest.

Footsteps signalled the two men's return. Followed what sounded like a debate. The Arab's voice became shrill, indignant, contrasting with McGash's hard, peremptory tones. McGash had the last word.

'A disagreement,' Gently whispered. 'I think the Arab may favour a dash for it. He's probably worked out the odds too and doesn't favour arguing them with the police.'

'Then perhaps ...'

'McGash won the argument. Cross your fingers he's made it stick.'

'You mean they would ... shoot us?'

'We're on the list. Perhaps it's time we arranged some sort of reception.'

He moved to the inner door, listened. From the door projected a step. Working silently, he laid cylindrical chumps on their sides along the step and over the area below it.

'Choose yourself a weapon.'

They selected their chumps. He placed himself on the side that the door would open. All was hushed again behind it, no murmur of words, no movement. Had he read that argument aright? Perhaps it was McGash who now favoured running. And the silence ... could it be the other door that suddenly would be flung open? He strained his ears in that direction: sound there must be when the peg was withdrawn. But sound there was none. And minutes ticked by. Time that now had to be on their side ...

At last a motion, a quick mutter, in the kitchen! He heard a step, the faint creak of a hinge. Someone in there had moved to a door, pushed it a little more open: like himself, stood listening. Listening, listening: in the enclosedness of the wood shed he could scarcely detect what to them must be plain: the murmur of engines. In fact what he first heard was a distant clumping of car doors.

'George ... ?'

'They're here.'

'Ah, thank heaven!'

But soon now the fun would begin.

'George, what are they doing?'

'Nothing,' Gently said. 'And they'll go on doing nothing as long as possible.'

'It is this battle of nerves?'

'They'll have taken up positions. But they won't make a move till Sinclair gets here. And he probably won't make a move either. They are going to leave the ball with McGash.'

'But ... if there is a deadline?'

'That's McGash's bluff. He's got to handle it when it comes.'

'George, it may not be I am so very brave.'

'McGash is on a deadline too,' Gently said. 'Empton. And Empton is no bluff.'

They had come back now from the door, were sitting again on the pile of chumps. After the little stir next door there had been few sounds for several minutes. Three cars had come down, Gently estimated, and were strung out at distances along the road.

Men equipped with guns, personal radios would be on the knoll, in the trees, down by the loch. One would be with the cars, watching the frontage, manning the transceiver. He'd be the only man in sight. McGash would have to guess about the rest.

A chance to start something? What the men didn't know was that the hostages weren't on the end of a gun. A quick rush now using grenades ... McGash wouldn't have time to pull them out of the wood shed. But mentally Gently shook his head. Grenades or not, there would be a slaughter. What they'd be rushing was a bolted door and a slit with two M52s firing through it ...

'Hold me my love.'

He took her in his arms.

'Suddenly I don't want to die.'

'It will never come to that.'

'My love, I feel cold, as though already I was in a grave.'

'Believe me,' he said. 'Believe me. McGash knows the game. He's a trained professional. He'll play out his hand but that's all. And when it's played out, he'll surrender.'

'I know only that he kills. And that terrible Arab.'

'Neither of them wants to provoke a shoot-out.'

'They will kill without thinking.'

'They'll have time to think. Think how to keep themselves alive.'

'Hold me tighter,' she sobbed.

He glanced at his watch: coming up to half after five. She hadn't a watch: he'd seen her bare wrist extended from the sleeve of the anorak.

'Soon Sinclair will be here. He's a wily bird.'

'Tell me about Sinclair,' Gabrielle said.

'I met him up here when he was just an Inspector. But he had the shrewdness to make use of me.'

'Tell me, tell me,' she said.

'I knew a local family. One of the sons had been a colleague of mine. They were concerned in a strange affair for which Sinclair was holding a young Canadian.'

'Yes, yes,' she said.

'The family was suspect, but they treated me as a friend. Sinclair more or less manoeuvred me into getting from them information they were witholding.'

'Go on, keep telling me,' she said.

'In the end the affair was sorted out. The Canadian married old Mackenzie's granddaughter, and Sinclair proved himself a very wise copper.'

'A wise copper,' she said.

'An able policeman. He'll know just how to handle McGash.'

'Yes,' she said. 'Yes, he'll know how.'

She burrowed her face deeper and deeper.

Fresh mutterings, movements, a soft click: then more slamming of car doors. It had to be Sinclair. Driving like the wind, he had made it in time out from Dornoch. Another two cars: there could be twenty men deployed or deploying about the house. Twenty: doubtless with more on the way. Twenty fingers for twenty triggers.

Suddenly from behind the door a shout:

'Stay right where you are, copper!'

Sinclair. He'd got from his car, had now come striding up to the gate.

'McGash.'

'You're talking to him.'

'So listen to me McGash,' Sinclair shouted. 'My name is Superintendent Sinclair, and I've got you surrounded. You'll put down your arms and walk out with your hands up.'

'Don't joke with me,' McGash shouted back. 'Did you get my message from the Frog, copper?'

'You heard me tell you,' Sinclair shouted. 'You're cornered, and I'm calling on you to surrender.'

'And I'm telling you,' McGash shouted. 'There's a girl here who's alive now, but won't be in twenty minutes. What's your answer to that, copper?'

'Put down your arms and walk out,' Sinclair shouted. 'That's my message to you, McGash.'

'Then her blood be on your conscience.'

No more from Sinclair. He'd said his piece perfectly. Now he'd be casually striding back to his car, a slow, contemptuous, uniformed figure.

'My love ...'

She was trembling violently, tears flooding from her eyes. He shook her.

'Believe me. You heard Sinclair. That's the way you've got to treat them.'

'He means it!'

'No. He's playing his bluff. Behind it he's as scared as you. You don't show fear because you've no need to. You treat them like the scum they are.'

'I am not brave—'

'No braveness called for. Just let them play out their little game.'

'George, they are killers!'

'Their teeth have been drawn. For their lives they dare not fire on you.'

She dabbed at the tears. 'Tell me what to do.'

'They'll stand you outside with a gun on you. Don't try to escape. Act as though you were bored, as though it were all some tiresome preliminary. It's a silly game, convincing nobody. If there's any gunplay, drop flat.'

'Will there be?'

'Not very likely. And it won't be directed at you.'

He found her a handkerchief. She wiped her face. Then she tucked the handkerchief in her anorak pocket. She wasn't trembling now. She held him by the arms and looked up into his face.

'In my town we remember Jeanne d'Arc. I am a daughter of Rouen. Kiss me this last time. I shall not disgrace my man.'

He bent to kiss her, and at that moment the bolts on the inner door were drawn. The door was flung wide. Behind their guns, McGash and the Arab stood, one supporting the other.

'A fine sight,' McGash said. 'Out, you bitch! You've a job to do for me. And you, Geordie. You'll see this. I wouldn't want the lesson wasted.'

'Then stand back, you lout,' Gabrielle said. 'Let me smell some fresh air.'

She marched through the doorway. She shoved the Arab aside. Gently followed. Hajjar struck him with his gun.

'So now, you pigs, what do you want?'

'I'm telling you,' McGash said. 'Oh I'm telling you.'

He had his gun hard in Gently's back. Hajjar's gun pointed at Gabrielle. Through the gap where the board had been removed one could see a single police car, fifty yards away. The outer door of the kitchen stood ajar. From the police car men were watching.

'You've got ten minutes,' McGash said. 'Just that, and then I'm blowing you away, you slut. You're going outside. You're going to talk to these coppers. And if they don't listen you're dead.'

'I may,' Gabrielle said.

'You'll do it, you bitch, if you want to live.'

'Don't think you're fooling anyone, McGash,' Gently said. 'You know, we know you're shooting nobody.'

McGash slammed him with the gun. 'Keep your trap shut.'

'Losing your nerve, McGash?' Gently said.

'Kick this bastard for me,' McGash said.

Hajjar aimed a kick at Gently's groin.

'Now one for her.'

The Arab kicked Gabrielle.

'Be told,' McGash said. 'Be told. This is real. She goes out there and ten minutes later her number's up. You hear me slut?'

'I hear,' Gabrielle said, 'a loudmouth. A frightened pig.'

'Out,' McGash snarled. 'Out. Just keep walking till I tell you to stop.'

Gabrielle looked at Gently. 'Do I humour this ape?'

'Oh, let him feel big,' Gently said.

'If you say so.' She shrugged, went through the doorway and walked ahead.

'Stop there!'

Gabrielle stopped. The Arab had gone to the gap at the window. He trained his gun on Gabrielle's back. One could hear his hoarse breathing.

'Start talking, slut!'

'But I have nothing to say.'

'You'd better think of something,' McGash said. 'Eight minutes is what you've got now. Those coppers have got to play ball by then.'

'I'll see if I can think of something.'

'Why bother to play it out?' Gently said. 'You're not going to shoot her, because you can't. The bluff was never on from the start.'

'You tricky bastard,' McGash said between his teeth. 'You've been getting at her haven't you? Kidding her along it's a bloody act, that she's going to walk out afterwards.'

'So it isn't an act?' Gently said.

'Not a bloody act,' McGash said. 'It goes on. Look at Dusty. I couldn't stop him now if I wanted.'

'You can stop him,' Gently said.

'Not short of blowing him away,' McGash said. 'This is Dusty's treat. He's psyched about women. He wets himself when he shoots them. So what about that?'

'You'll stop him,' Gently said.

'Watch me,' McGash said. 'Bloody watch me. You've made a mistake, copper. I can get by with you on a gun.'

'He'll be shooting you,' Gently said, 'if he shoots her.'

'Now close your trap,' McGash said. 'And watch.'

He bored with the gun. They stood back from the door, looking out at Gabrielle, the car, the men. The men had got out of the car. One was Sinclair. He came forward to the gate.

'Hold it!' McGash shouted. 'She gets it else.'

Sinclair halted at the gate.

'You'd better give up now, McGash,' he shouted. 'We don't want accidents with the girl.'

McGash laughed savagely. 'Who's talking of accidents? Are you ready to give me my car and plane?'

'I don't have authority for that,' Sinclair shouted.

'Then bloody get authority,' McGash shouted back. 'Get on your blower. You've got five minutes. You see her alive, you'll see her dead.'

'Let's talk about it,' Sinclair shouted.

'Five minutes,' McGash shouted. 'And no more chat.'

'Let me come up to the house.'

'If you do you stop a bullet.'

Sinclair made a gesture of futility. But he went back to his car. The gun on Gently's spine shifted slightly, jabbed firm.

'Another tricky copper,' McGash said. 'But he'll see. He'll see.'

'Suppose he does what you want,' Gently asked. 'What then?'

'You're bloody posthumous,' McGash said. 'Shut up.'

Still Gabrielle was standing relaxed, indifferent, one leg crooked, one straight. She had hands clasped before her, apparently was staring at the hills. At the gap Hajjar crouched motionless, his eyes never leaving her back. His rough breathing came in starts; he held his gun with both hands.

'Four minutes!' McGash shouted.

Near the door stood one of the wood chumps. Grey, stripped of bark, it had probably served as a stop. Four feet away. Gently shifted weight from foot to foot, edged closer. The gun followed.

He moved again. The gun jabbed painfully.

'Kick it, Geordie.'

Gently stayed still.

'Kick it, you bastard!' McGash snarled. 'Kick it through the door. And while you're at it, hear me tell you I'm on first pressure.'

Gently moved to the chump. The gun moved with him. He kicked the chump through the doorway. The chump rolled to a stop beside Gabrielle. Gabrielle stared at it, elaborately shrugged.

'That's better, Geordie,' McGash said. 'Don't start getting naughty thoughts at this stage. You're right, I may be nervous, may hoik this trigger before I'm fit.'

'I thought you were a professional, monsieur,' Gabrielle said.

'Wrap up, you cow!' McGash snarled.

'Can it be that you are really so timid?'

'Two minutes,' McGash said. He shouted: 'Two minutes!'

Gabrielle sighed boredly and folded her arms. She began to hum the Marseillaise. Gently could feel a tremor in the gun. But nothing changed in the aspect of the Arab.

'Listen!' McGash shouted. 'One bloody minute – then you'll be wishing you'd spoken sooner. Can you hear me?'

Sinclair could hear him. But he sat tight in the car.

'This is your last chance, you sod.'

Sinclair wasn't even looking towards him.

'Then it's on your head, you bastard. You're responsible for what happens now.'

But something was stirring in the car: from the back a man wearing a blazer got out. Frénaye! He spoke a few words to Sinclair, then turned and walked towards the gate.

'Monsieur McGash?'

Gently felt the gun jog.

'Back off, Froggie, or I'll shoot you down.'

'Monsieur, I wish to have words with you.'

'I'm telling you,' McGash shouted. 'I'm telling you.'

But Frénaye paid no heed. He kept coming. He came through the gate, began to cross the grass. As though picking his way he moved off to the right, wide of Gabrielle and the door.

'Just one more step!' McGash shouted.

Frénaye's gait didn't falter.

'Monsieur McGash,' Gabrielle said. 'I feel suddenly faint, I would like to sit down.'

'Stand up, you whore!'

Hajjar's breathing was ragged. His gun wavered, pulled away towards Frénaye. At the same moment Gently felt the gun behind him withdraw from his back. In his life he'd never moved faster. His hands clamped over McGash's hand and the gun. His finger crushed down on McGash's finger just as Hajjar spun round from the window. The gun crashed. The high velocity bullet struck Hajjar in the face. His skull blew. Headless, the body fell down, gouting blood.

'You bugger ... you bugger ...!'

McGash had his arm round Gently's neck. He was forcing Gently's head down to the muzzle of the gun, wrenching to free the finger on the trigger. Then something violent struck him. He grunted, went heavy, slid down. Big-eyed, Gabrielle stood there. She was holding the wood chump and breathing fast.

'Have I—killed him?'

'You haven't killed him.'

McGash's wig hung askew. Under it, sandy hair through which blood was beginning to well.

'Come ... get out of here.'

He hustled her through the door. Men came running. Sinclair came. Frénaye was sitting on the grass, looking sick.

'Man, are you all right?' Sinclair said.

'Both all right,' Gently said.

'And he's alive?'

'McGash is alive.'

'Jings, jings, what a turn-up,' Sinclair said.

He stared at Frénaye. Frénaye's face was white.

'Ach to goodness,' Sinclair said. 'I've seen men show nerve monsieur, but never before the like of that.'

'Is there a hotel we can go to,' Gently said.

'Aye,' Sinclair said. 'Aye, at Tongue. Take my car.'

'Thanks,' Gently said.

He took Gabrielle's arm; they went to the cars.

Frénaye went with them, travelling in front with Sinclair's driver. Until the car moved off, Gabrielle remained stiff, eyes averted from the house and the policemen. Then she fell into a tremble and began to sob. Gently held her to him, saying nothing. Nobody said anything. They crept on by Loch Hope and at last turned right into the vast of A'Mhoine. Slowly her trembling, sobbing ceased; she wiped her eyes and sat straighter. She looked up for a time at Gently, then at the savage moors they were crossing.

'This place ... what is its name, my friend?'

'What do they call it?' Gently asked the driver.

'They call it A'Mhoine,' the driver said. 'The hill over there is Ben Loyal.'

'Do people live here?' Gabrielle asked.

'Not a single soul,' the driver said. 'You'll see one house, but it was never lived in. It was shelter for the men who built the road.'

'My God, what a country!' Gabrielle said. She sighed and was silent again. She took Gently's hand; sometimes she looked at him, sometimes at the wastes of A'Mhoine. In front Frénaye stared straight ahead and the eyes of the driver stayed with the road.

At last they crossed a great kyle at the mouth of which were islands, ascended a gentle rise and arrived at a village. At a hotel the driver parked; he went in ahead to make arrangements. Drinks, sandwiches were brought to a private lounge; then the manageress came smilingly to Gabrielle.

'Madame is about my size ...?'

'Oh madame!' Gabrielle said. 'You will save my life.' T Gently she said: 'Alas my friend, but so soon I must leave you again.'

When she had gone Frénaye looked at Gently.

'Monsieur, but that woman has courage,' he said.

'She had need of it,' Gently said. 'It was she most of all who put down McGash.'

'All is now well between you.'

'All is well.'

'Monsieur is a lucky man,' Frénaye said. 'I too have such a woman for my own. It is happiness beyond all purchase.'

'We are two lucky men,' Gently said.

'I will drink to that,' Frénaye said.

They drank to it.

'Monsieur,' Frénaye said. 'This unpleasant Empton is on his way here. Advice was of course passed to Inverness where unluckily it came to his attention. I understand there were exchanges with the excellent Sinclair which the latter saw fit to ignore. I assume that Monsieur Empton will now seek to take charge of the affair.'

Gently drank. 'He'll be lucky,' he said.

'That was indeed my impression. The excellent Sinclair murmured words which my modest English failed to comprehend. Yet this Empton has the authority?'

'We'll see,' Gently said. 'He's in Sutherland, not in Whitehall.'

'That will be different?' Frénaye said.

'That will be different.'

Frénaye shrugged and took a sandwich.

Cars pulled up. Sinclair entered; he went straight to the tray and poured a drink. Tall, lanky, with long, lined features, he took a gulp before speaking.

'Ach then! So far, so good. McGash is on his way to Peterhead jail. How is the lady?'

'Taking a bath,' Gently said. 'Which way have you sent McGash?'

'Not through Lairg,' Sinclair said. His eye twinkled. 'I've been having a chat with Guthrie,' he said. 'There'll be no hijacking of prisoners on my patch – nor yet in his, I'm thinking.' He drank. 'But you, man,' he said. 'You've got a reception waiting down yonder. That chiel Barentin has been stirring things up – I would not put it past a civic reception.'

Gently grimaced. 'Thanks for the warning.'

'Aye, but it goes further,' Sinclair said. 'He's under the impression there's a wedding in the offing, he's about lending you châteaux, Rolls-Royces and that sort of chattel. Any truth in the rumour, man?'

'Let us say it is premature,' Gently said.

Sinclair eyed him. 'Just premature,' he said. 'Well, it's maybe over soon to be pushing such questions. That was no picnic down the glen.'

'No picnic at all,' Gently said.

'You did well to hasten her away from it,' Sinclair said. 'Jings man, you never saw the like of that Arab.'

He poured more whisky, drank. Nobody said anything for a time. From the window one saw the four peaks of Ben Loyal, luridly lit by evening sun. Then, more distant, the hump of Ben Hope, summit streaming bloody cloud; and in the foreground the kyle and the ruin of a watchtower on a knoll.

Gabrielle returned.

'My friend ... I have not been so very long?'

She stood before them shyly, dressed in borrowed skirt and jumper. Her golden brown hair was brushed, her cheeks still glowing from the towel; even the bruised eye seemed fainter, its lividity softened by bathing. She smiled at the three men getting to their feet. But her eyes were only for Gently.

'My gosh lassie,' Sinclair said, 'but you're looking a different woman now.'

'Mademoiselle,' Frénaye said. 'For such a transformation Madame Frénaye would have needed two hours.'

'And you?' Gabrielle said to Gently.

Gently said nothing; he placed a chair for her.

'Well now, well now,' Sinclair said. 'Let me speak a little and have done. I'm wishful to shake your hand, lassie, and I shall be a proud man doing it. And that's all for that, since I'll be making a fool of myself if I say more.'

'Monsieur I am touched,' Gabrielle said.

'Now as to business—' Sinclair began.

He was interrupted by a knock; a constable appeared at the door.

'Sir, a Superintendent Empton is wanting words with you.'

'Is he now,' Sinclair said. 'That should be interesting. Show him in man – let's see the colour of his face.'

A moment later Empton entered. He closed the door. He stared at them.

'Right then,' Empton said. 'Roy of The Rovers has done his act. Sorry to break it up and all that, old man, but the time has come to let in the professionals. Where's McGash?'

Gently nodded to Sinclair.

'So where's McGash?' Empton repeated.

Sinclair gazed at him with puckered eyes. 'I would not just be certain of that,' he said.

'Then you'd better be certain,' Empton said. 'My writ runs in these parts, old man. I have a plane standing by at Wick airport and when it leaves I want McGash on board it.'

'Now that's sad,' Sinclair said. 'Not to mention a great waste of taxpayers' money. McGash is on his way to Peterhead, and I cannot just say where you can light upon him.'

Empton glared at him. He pulled up a chair and sat down face to face with Sinclair.

'Listen jock,' he said. 'You're not dealing with an amateur. I can have you suspended at the drop of a hat. I'm the man who says jump, and you don't ask when but how high. And McGash is my prisoner, are you hearing me, jock? He's mine and I'll have him. So get on that telephone.'

'Ach well,' Sinclair said. 'You're a forceful mannie. But what for should I be handing him over to you? There sits the man who felt his collar, and I'm hearing nothing about planes and Wick airport from him.'

'On the blower,' Empton said. 'And quick, jock. Or you'll answer for it with your rank. McGash is state property. He's my property. The Frogs want him for conspiracy, kidnap and murder.'

'Is that so,' Sinclair said. 'Man, there's a coincidence. He's wanted in Scotland for the very same things. Along with illegal entry, criminal assault, vehicle theft and malicious damage. We'll have to get together with the French,' Sinclair said, 'to see who'll have the privilege of giving him lodging. But man, I do not hear he's committed crimes in England – unless maybe it was over-flying Buckingham Palace.'

'Right,' Empton said. 'Entertainment over. Do I get him, or do I get you?'

'Aye,' Sinclair said. 'It's a ticklish question. But I think he's best kept in responsible hands.'

'Then it's your funeral, jock.'

'Maybe,' Sinclair said. 'And yet, I cannot help wondering, man. When you've made such a botch of your job up here, will your bosses down in London be for taking you seriously?'

Empton sprang up. 'Listen!'

'Hush man, hush,' Sinclair said. 'You'll be startling the lady – though truth to tell she showed few nerves when she was handling McGash. Where were you then?'

'You'll pay,' Empton said. 'You'll pay for this, jock.'

'And then again,' Sinclair said. 'When she was rescuing Barentin – what were you doing up Moriston, man?'

'I was tricked into it!' Empton snarled.

'Aye, there was trickery somewhere,' Sinclair said. 'You set a trap for a brother officer and got hoisted in it yourself. What sort of a policeman do they call you? I'm telling you, you're laughing stock in Scotland. You're a joke man. They're splitting their tunics from Balnakiel to Berwick Law. And I'm to hand over my prisoner to you? To a music-hall turn spitting fire and brimstone? On your way, man – on your way – or I'll put you inside for insulting behaviour.'

'You're suspended,' Empton bawled. 'And I have the authority.'

'You, you have nothing,' Sinclair said. 'Except maybe a fool's cap, and that you brought with you from London.' He called the constable. 'Show this laddie out, and see you point him towards England.'

'You'll pay – the whole boiling of you!' Empton shouted.

'This way sir,' the constable said. He took Empton's arm.

Sinclair was making clucking noises in his throat. He wiped his eyes and poured another drink. 'Ach well,' he said. 'It's a sad heart – but I shall not soon forget Glen Moriston!' He spluttered over his glass. 'But to business,' he said. 'It is ourselves who should be stirring too. The Press will have wind of this affair, and you'd best be other wheres than at Tongue. Will you away with me to Dornoch?'

Soon after eight they were back in the cars. They drove through the long evening. Gabrielle slept on Gently's arm.

Frénaye left them the next morning.

At Dornoch the sun had returned; they walked on the beach and then lay down to bask and listen to the rustle of the combers. Somewhere else reports were being made, interrogations taken, statements given; but Sinclair hadn't bothered them. Yesterday's world was far from Dornoch's Sunday beach.

Gabrielle had slept late and was still sleepy. For a spell she dozed in the mild sun. Gently sat by, pipe in mouth, now and then tossing pebbles in the sea. Small birds ran and retreated at the tideline; further out sailed the terns, the gulls. A white painted ship, low, without funnels, was slowly inscribing the sea's rim. Gabrielle stirred and sighed.

'My friend …?'

No one was near. He kissed her.

'My friend, when shall we marry?'

'At once,' Gently said, kissing her again.

'You will get leave?'

'Immediately.'

'Shall it be in France?'

'In France,' he said.

'And we will invite', she said, 'Monsieur Frénaye. And the brother-in-law who paints. And the sister who is crazed by Proust. And—'

'All of these,' Gently said. 'Barentin has offered us his car and château.'

'Oh,' Gabrielle said. She scooped up sand, let it leak through her fingers.

'You do not want a Rolls-Royce and a château?' Gently said.

'Perhaps I am a foolish woman,' she said. 'When I am dreaming it is just you and I in my little car. Driving south. Did we not do it once before?'

'We did it once before,' he said.

'But oh,' she said, 'it was so short – just Honfleur to Lisieux. When I was wishing it would go on for ever.'

'Then we will do it again,' he said.

'You do not wish for this Rolls-Royce either?'

'I do not wish for it,' Gently said. 'Just your little car. When we are married.'

'This is certain,' she said, 'not the car nor the château?'

'Neither,' Gently said. 'What trash they buy with money.'

'Tell me again when we shall be married.'

Kissing her, Gently said: 'Not long.'